Wyoming Showdown

Fifteen years earlier, Matthew Granger had been put on a stagecoach heading east by his father. From that day Granger had never looked back. Over the years he'd managed to survive in a dangerous business and was now a rich man. His return to Springwater was a final visit to settle family affairs.

He planned to be back in Boston as fast as he could, but he soon found it wasn't that easy. Old enemies were still around. Thomas Ralston, owner of the Lazy Y, was taking over the town and settling scores with the Granger family along the way.

Matthew Granger was a target once more. Strapping on his Navy Colt, he knew Boston would have to wait.

By the same author

Lannigan's Star
Stage to Cheyenne
Shadow of the Gun

Wyoming Showdown

JACK EDWARDES

A Black Horse Western

ROBERT HALE · LONDON

© Jack Edwardes 2006
First published in Great Britain 2006

ISBN-10: 0-7090-8195-2
ISBN-13: 978-0-7090-8195-1

Robert Hale Limited
Clerkenwell House
Clerkenwell Green
London EC1R 0HT

Typeset by
Derek Doyle & Associates, Shaw Heath
Printed and bound in Great Britain by
Antony Rowe Limited, Wiltshire

CHAPTER ONE

The riders had appeared about an hour after the stage to Springwater had changed horses. Granger reckoned they were maybe three miles distant on higher ground, riding in a tight bunch, making it difficult for him to decide how many there were. At least four, he reckoned, maybe more. Just harmless cowboys, he'd told himself, when he first saw them. But he was no longer sure. There was something about the bunch keeping pace with the stage that made him uneasy.

He should try and relax more, he decided. Maybe the bad news he'd received from Springwater, and the loss of two men on his last job were getting to him. Start suspecting everyone and folks would think him some pilgrim ready to jump at his own shadow.

A bath, a good meal, and a soft bed would soon put him right. His journey from Boston had been a long one. This last leg of his journey since leaving the U.P. railroad had dragged on for a couple of days. He turned his head to look again towards the distant higher ground. The riders, he saw, were still keeping pace with the stage.

'Has something caught your attention, Mr Granger?'

The speaker, white-haired and wearing grey bombazine, was the elderly wife of the Reverend Dunning.

She and her husband, with their young granddaughter, had joined the stage at the last station. The reverend, despite the early hour, appeared to be dozing in a corner seat, his head against the leather curtains.

'Nothing to concern you, ma'am,' Granger said. 'A bunch of riders, that's all.'

'Ranchhands, I guess,' said the young Englishman who, from his clothes, looked sorely in need of funds. He'd spent most of the journey scribbling furiously in a pocket-sized notebook. His name, Granger had learned, was Roberts.

'They're probably going to the Ralston spread,' Roberts added.

'They're not bad men, are they?' asked the Dunning grandchild, still young enough to have her hair down.

Her grandmother leaned across to pat the girl's hand. 'Now, Polly, you mustn't worry. All those stories you've heard about Indians and hold-up men. Why, that was all when your poor departed mother was a little girl.'

The reverend opened his eyes and shifted his shoulders to sit up straighter against the cushions. He looked a little guilty. 'You're right, my dear,' he said after a moment. 'When Mr Ralston set up the Lazy Y eighteen years ago his men chased all the no-goods out of the county.'

His wife's mouth set in a firm line. 'That may be true, Mr Dunning, but I've had it on good account that some of Mr Ralston's men are no better than the no-goods they chased away.'

She turned back to Granger who was again staring intently towards the higher ground. The bunch of riders had split up. At least two must have veered away, dropping below the skyline out of Granger's view. The remaining two had moved closer, now maybe only a mile or so distant from the trail.

'Do you know Springwater, Mr Granger?'

Granger paused a moment before replying. The Englishman was probably right. The riders were already on Ralston's payroll or they were cowboys heading out to the Lazy Y looking for work. During his stop-over in Cheyenne, Granger had heard that the big cattle-drives south for the railhead would be starting in the next couple of days.

He turned back and smiled at the elderly woman. 'I was born there, ma'am. I went East fifteen years ago.'

'And what brings you back—' She broke off suddenly, her face showing concern. 'Oh, my! You poor man! You're Sheriff Granger's son?'

'Yes, ma'am.'

The words were barely out his mouth when Granger, along with the other four passengers, reached out a hand for support as the stage suddenly accelerated. There was a loud shout from the driver, the crack of a whip, and the thrumming of hoofs on the packed soil of the trail. The stage swayed from side to side as if it were a paper boat tossed around by waves.

Granger recognized the sharp crack of a long gun followed by the deep bark of a scatter-gun sounding above his head. An instant later again came the crack of a long gun. There was a shout of pain and something heavy clattered against the side of the stage. Granger guessed the tall Swede riding shotgun had been hit, and had dropped his weapon. The stage began to slow, and Granger heard the sounds of approaching horses.

Granger inwardly cursed his decision to stow his sidearm in his boxes.

'Anyone with a weapon?'

Roberts and the reverend shook their heads. Mrs Dunning had lost colour, her face as white as the hair that

7

peeped from below the brim of her bonnet. She held Polly's hand in both her own, trying to comfort the girl whose face was pinched with fear.

'Stay calm, and do what they say,' Granger ordered. 'Give them what you have if they demand it. That way we all get to live another day.'

Roberts exploded. 'I'll be damned if I—'

'You'll do as you're told,' interrupted Granger harshly. 'I ain't gettin' killed for your hurt feelin's.'

There was more shouting from the driver and the stage gradually slowed until it eased to a halt. For a moment the only sound was the blowing and snorting of the horses, and the thud of a hoof being stamped against the hard dirt of the trail. The door of the stage was flung open.

'Everybody out!'

A man, Colt in hand, stood back from the stage. His face was uncovered, several days' stubble showing against his sallow skin. His trail clothes were streaked in dirt, and the toes of his boots were marked with dried mud. As Granger stepped down to the trail he saw to his right the second *bandido* astride a big sorrel, holding in his left hand the reins of a parrot-mouthed roan. In his right hand he held a Winchester, the long gun nestling across his saddle, the barrel pointing in Granger's direction.

Behind Granger, the Dunnings and their granddaughter stepped down from the stage. Finally, as Granger moved a pace to stand in front of Polly, Roberts appeared, his head held high, anger sparkling in his blue eyes. The *bandido* looked at the assembled passengers, his eyes settling on Granger.

'Well now, what we got here? A dude from back East, I reckon. Let's see that fancy coat open, dude.'

Granger unbuttoned his coat to show he was unarmed. Satisfied, the *bandido* scratched his stubble with the barrel of his Colt in mock thoughtfulness. 'OK, we got two old-timers an'—'

The rider spat into the dust. 'We come for the mailbag, Frank!'

'Shut your goddamned mouth! I'm gettin' to it!'

The *bandido* called Frank had turned to glance up at the rider, and Granger tensed, seeing a chance. But quickly Frank turned back to face the little group at the side of the stage and the moment passed. Frank shouted up at the driver.

'Throw down the mailbag!'

The driver, a grizzled old man in his sixties wearing a red mackinaw, squirted tobacco on to the trail from between blackened teeth. He kept one hand on the arm of the big Swede who had slumped back in his seat, his eyes closed.

'An' if I don't?'

A leer grew slowly on the face of the man called Frank. He raised his arm and Granger heard the metallic click of the Colt being cocked.

'Throw it down,' Granger called. 'No sense in gettin' anybody killed.'

Frank chuckled loudly. 'The dude's got brains, old man! Now throw it down!'

There was a snort of fury from Roberts as the driver, after reaching behind his feet, threw down the mailbag where it landed a couple of paces from Frank's feet.

Frank shifted sideways and brought his Colt around to aim at the group of passengers. He bent to pick up the mailbag. As he stood up, his eyes came to rest on Polly, as if noticing her for the first time.

'Now ain't we got ourselves a nice plump chicken!'

A strangled noise came from Roberts. 'You touch one hair on Miss Polly's head, and you'll have me to answer to!'

For a moment there was absolute silence. Then Frank slowly raised his Colt, aiming directly at the Englishman. He turned his head slightly to address the rider.

'I'm jest gonna—'

The throwing knife, sprung from the leather armstrap concealed beneath Granger's coat sleeve, struck the *bandido* one inch below his ear, the force of Granger's throw burying the blade to the hilt. The *bandido* sank to his knees, blood gushing from his throat, and pitched forward, face down.

Behind Granger there were screams from Mrs Dunning and the girl.

'What the hell!'

The rider brought up his Winchester. In that instant Granger could see only the mouth of the barrel as black as doom. There was a roar of fury as Roberts flung himself forward, his arms outstretched. His hands closed around the barrel of the long gun, forcing it high and away from the group as the *bandido* pulled the trigger. There was a sharp crack as the slug went harmlessly high in the air, above and beyond the stagecoach. With a jerk of his muscular arms Roberts pulled the man from his saddle, forcing the man to the ground where he landed with a bone-shaking thud. Granger took two swift paces and swung his leg. Boot leather smashed against an ear and the *bandido* became still.

Granger bent quickly and slid the *bandido's* sidearm from its holster. He picked up the long gun, and seeing the hilt protruding from the man's boot-top heaved out a knife and hurled it into the bunch and buffalo grass away from the trail. Granger and Roberts stood still, drawing in deep breaths, staring at each other. Then they both turned to the others.

Mrs Dunning had swooned away, her limp body fallen

back against her husband, who stood, ashen-faced, supporting her. Polly had slumped to the ground, weeping quietly, not caring that her blue cotton dress was amongst the dirt. Gently, Roberts reached down, and helped her to her feet.

'Everything is fine now, Polly,' he said soothingly. 'You're quite safe now.'

Granger stepped aside to look up at the driver. 'The shotgun gonna make it, Josh?'

'He's a danged lucky feller. Got creased by that no-good, but he'll be OK.' Josh spat between the hoofs of the wheelers. 'Dangest move I ever saw with a knife, mister. I'm much obliged.'

'Get the Swede inside,' ordered Granger.

He turned to Roberts who was helping the revived Mrs Dunning to board the stage. 'You OK ridin' shotgun into town, Mr Roberts?'

'I can do that.' Roberts pointed back along the trail. 'The scatter-gun's back there. I'll see the ladies onboard first.'

The Reverend Dunning was looking down at the dead *bandido*, his lips moving with silent words. He looked up at Granger.

'What happens to this man?'

Granger bent to pull out the knife from the man's throat, walked to the side of the trail, and wiped the blade on a tuft of grass. He returned to stand by the dead man.

'We'll put both these no-goods on the roan. I'll ride the sorrel.'

'It's a bad business for any man to lose his life,' Dunning said sombrely. 'But I guess he'd have taken Polly, an' maybe killed us all.'

'Why don't you get onboard, Reverend? The Swede's gonna need some help. Mr Roberts will give me a hand here.'

11

'Thank you for saving us, Mr Granger.'

Granger nodded, then turned away to take up the loose reins of the roan, and lead the horse alongside the body. As the scent of blood rose to its nostrils the animal jerked its head away, but Granger had expected this, and he leaned back, digging a heel into the ground. He waited until the roan had steadied before placing the long gun on the ground. Then he unlashed the saddle strings holding the length of hemp to the rig. Dropping to one knee he took the dally-end of the rope, secured it around the dead man's boots and tied a bowline.

'You gonna give me a hand here, Mr Roberts?' Granger said as the Englishman stepped down from the stage.

The two men hoisted the body level with the saddle as close to the cantle as possible. A raised hoof and slight shake of the head were the animal's only movements as the two men, at Granger's nod, heaved the body across the back of the horse.

Helped by Roberts, Granger passed the rope beneath the horse's belly a couple of times before lashing the rope around the body. Finally he secured the remaining length to the rear of the stage.

'OK, Mr Roberts. You get the scatter-gun, an' I'll get this trail-trash on his feet.'

He picked up the Winchester and walked across to where the second *bandido* lay on his back without moving, his eyes closed. Granger stared down at him for a few seconds. Then he kicked him hard in the ribs.

'On your feet, *cabron!*'

Granger kicked him again, and the man groaned and stirred, attempting to rise from the ground. Granger leaned forward, took the man's trail-shirt in his bunched fist, and hauled him to his feet. Ignoring the man's protests, Granger dragged him to the roan.

12

'Get in the saddle. You're gonna have the pleasure o' takin' Frank on his last ride. You fall off, an' I'll tie you to the stage an' drag you into town.'

Once the man's hands had taken the reins, Granger swiftly tied his wrists with a saddle string. He turned to watch Roberts, scatter-gun in hand, climbing up alongside the driver, then he took up the reins of the sorrel and swung into the saddle, the Winchester resting in front of him.

'OK, Josh! Let's roll 'em!'

As the stage moved forward, the rope from the rear of the stage tautened, and the roan stepped out. Satisfied that the *bandido* had a firm grasp of the reins, Granger urged his mount forward before abruptly swinging around in the saddle. From the high ground to the west something had flashed in the afternoon sun.

A spyglass, maybe? He'd seen at least four riders earlier in the day. Did the two *bandidos* belong to that bunch? If so, why hadn't the others also attacked the stage? Granger breathed in deeply. Something was going on here he hadn't yet got a handle on.

CHAPTER TWO

Twenty yards down Springwater's Main Street Granger saw a small knot of people gathering outside the stagecoach office. The arrival of the stage was always the cue for a few townsfolk to gather. Who knows who might be coming into town? But as the townsfolk became aware of the two horses behind the stage, and the load one was carrying, men and women flooded on to the boardwalks lining both sides of the street. The murmur of their voices rose to an excited chatter as the stage rolled over the hardpack.

Granger took his first look around his home town for almost fifteen years. The town had grown bigger; many more stores lined the street which seemed much longer than he remembered. But there were signs of hard times. Here and there a store-front was boarded up as if the owner had thrown in his hand and left town.

The men on the boardwalks were mainly dressed in working clothes, protected by dusty aprons. One or two men wore city clothes. Most of the women wore plain cotton dresses, their skirts sweeping the boards. Here and there more prosperous-looking women wore fashionable dresses, probably shipped from back East, high-button boots showing beneath their hems.

By the time the stage had drawn to a halt a large crowd had gathered and Granger was forced to urge his mount forward so as to move alongside the stage. Shouted questions from the crowd rang out, but Granger ignored them.

'Mr Roberts!' Granger called. 'I'll go see the sheriff. Have my stuff taken down to the Majestic. Get a room yourself there when you've done that.'

'I'll gladly take care of your boxes, Mr Granger.' Roberts shrugged broad shoulders. 'But I can't afford to stay in the hotel.'

'Tell them I'm good for it,' said Granger.

Without waiting for an answer, he handed up to Josh, the driver, the Winchester he'd been carrying. 'Sheriff's office still past the blacksmith?'

'Sure is, Mr Granger.'

Granger turned his mount, and moved to the rear of the stage. Leaning down from his saddle, he freed the rope securing the roan. The *bandido* hadn't moved since the stage had halted, sitting slumped in the saddle, his head down. Granger, rope in hand, turned his horse's head, and pushed through the crowd, the roan a few paces behind. There were cries of horror from some of the women who had only emerged from the stores when the stage had halted. They backed away, not having seen until then, through the press of people, the bloody body of a dead man.

Halfway down the street a couple of cowhands on wiry quarterhorses reined in to watch Granger ride by. Over to his left a blacksmith stepped out from the flames and steam of his forge, sweat gleaming on his face.

'You sure brought a load back home, Matthew Granger!'

Granger raised his hand in recognition. 'Talk to you later, Sam!'

Another fifty yards down the street Granger reached the sheriff's office. A young man, his clothes covered in a paint-stained apron, was brushing whitewash on to the timbers of a side wall. His head was protected from splashes by a large floppy hat. At first he paid no attention to the arrival of the two horses, intent on his work. But as Granger reined in he put down the brush into a bucket, and looked in Granger's direction.

'My, oh my! What in tarnation you got there?'

'Sheriff around?' Granger asked.

To Granger's surprise, the young man ducked his head to slip off his apron, revealing the shiny sheriff's star pinned to his shirt.

'That's me!' He pulled off the floppy hat, and Granger could see his features for the first time.

'Young Billy! What the hell you doin' with that badge?'

The young man stepped forward, his eyes screwed up against the evening sun. 'Jumpin' rattlesnakes! Matthew! Didn't know you in them fancy clothes. You heard about Pa?' His attention shifted to the roan.

'An' what you got here?'

'These no-goods tried to hold up the stage.'

Billy let out a low whistle. 'An' they say lightnin' don' strike twice! Mr Ralston ain't gonna like this at all!' He turned on his heel. 'Hank!'

A moment later a skinny man who'd seen at least seventy summers appeared from the office. His bib overalls were heavily patched. An old straw hat topped his heavily lined forehead, a bulbous nose, and a whiskery chin. When he caught sight of the dead man his Adam's apple bobbed a couple of times.

'Take the dead 'un 'cross to Moses Jackson. Town'll have to bury him.' Billy ordered. 'Hoss can go to the livery.'

He took a short knife from his belt and stepped down to cut through the saddle strings binding the *bandido's* hands, before moving back.

'Get down, an' no tricks. You're goin' in the cage.'

He watched the *bandido* dismount. Then, apparently satisfied that there'd be no trouble, he looked up at Granger. 'There's coffee on the stove. I'll get this no-good bedded down.'

Ten minutes later Granger was seated in a high-backed chair by Billy's ink-stained desk when the young man reappeared from out back. He helped himself to coffee before crossing the office to sit behind the desk opposite Granger.

'So tell me what went on.'

Granger took another sip of the hot black coffee before replying. His young stepbrother wearing the sheriff's badge was taking some getting used to. He'd expected to find a man by the name of Jenkins. And Billy's remark about two attempted hold-ups also made him pause. Had that son of a bitch Ralston such a powerful grip on the county that crime around these parts was considered unusual? He trusted Billy, but he'd been in situations like this many times. Before he told Billy all he was thinking he'd find out more of what was going on in Springwater.

For several minutes Granger gave a plain account of the attempt on the stage, downplaying his own role, emphasizing the bravery of the Englishman, Roberts. He said nothing about his suspicions that the whole incident had probably been watched from the high ground. And why, he suddenly wondered, had the no-good now in the cage felt the need to remind his partner about the mailbag? When Granger had finished, Billy nodded.

'Judge Parker'll be here next month,' he said. 'He'll handle it.'

Granger reached into his coat pocket and pulled out a small leather case. Opening it, he offered it to Billy. 'You use these?'

Billy looked at the neat row of ready-made cigarettes. 'Now ain't that a treat. Bankin' business is sure doin' you proud.'

'Tell me about Pa,' Granger said, when he'd lit both cigarettes.

Billy's expression became sombre. 'Dangest thing, Matt. After Pa retired, he useta spend coupla mornin's every week takin' coffee with Mr Rogers over at the dry goods.'

Granger nodded. 'Walter Rogers wrote me about that.'

'Anyways, one mornin' three no-goods attacked the bank. There was a shot, an' Pa musta forgot for a moment he'd taken off the badge. He went rushin' into the street. The three were comin' outa the bank. There was a shootout. The three were shot dead but Pa got cut down.'

'Where the hell was Jenkins?'

'Outa town. When he got back he packed his rig and skedaddled. He told folks he hadn't taken the job to go up against bank-robbers.'

Granger looked at Billy's shirt. 'So how come you're wearin' the badge?'

'Folks weren't willin' to take it on. The town ain't like it was when you were here. Men here got families an' steady jobs. They ain't keen on mixin' it with drunk cowboys. For a coupla weeks the town was without a sheriff. The councilmen were talkin' about askin' for help from the county sheriff. Then Mr Ralston said if I'd do the job he'd see I'd get elected.'

'That's damned odd,' Granger said. What was Ralston up to?

'Sure was,' Billy said. 'Pa was always doin' his best to keep Mr Ralston from dictatin' what went on in this town.' Billy shrugged. 'But you know what it's like in the damned sawmill. I ain't keen on coughin' up dust for the rest of my life. An' this job pays eighty a month an' a dollar bonus for each drunk I haul outa the saloon.'

Granger nodded, keeping his thoughts to himself, but maybe Billy taking over the badge wasn't a bad idea. One Granger killed upholding the law, another given the chance to step into his boots. Although he could never forgive Ralston, maybe the rancher had changed in fifteen years.

Granger stood up. 'I'm gonna get cleaned up over at the Majestic, then I'll ride out an' see Katy and Jack.'

Billy shifted his eyes, looking uncomfortable. 'It ain't that easy.'

Granger frowned. 'What's the problem?'

The young man licked his lips seeming to search for the right words to say. 'It's like this, Mat—' he said finally, his voice tailing away.

'Out with it, Billy!'

'Jack and Katy ain't at Pa's old place no more. Jack got into debt with the bank. Coupla weeks after Pa got killed, Mr Ralston bought his paper from the bank and called the debt in. Jack couldn't pay, and Mr Ralston had him move out.'

Granger swore loudly. For a moment there he'd been willing to give Ralston the benefit of the doubt. But the son of a bitch hadn't changed. He must have been waiting for Pa to be out of the way so he could make his move. Taking over the Granger homestead would be one way of getting revenge for all the times Pa had stood up to him. His own journey back to Boston from South Virginia and the onward rail and stagecoach journey to Springwater had taken him over a month. He knew now that every day had been worth it.

'What the hell would Ralston want with a homestead this side of the river? An' where's Katy now?'

'I dunno, Matt. The place is still empty.' Billy looked even more awkward. 'Katy and Jack are workin' in the saloon. I've given 'em some money, but I ain't exactly rich.'

'Katy in the goddamned Nugget! Has Jack gone crazy?' Granger snatched up his silver grey Dakota hat from the desk, and crossed the room. As he opened the door he turned back to his stepbrother.

'You listen to me, Billy! Ralston never made a damned move ever, without lookin' to gain somethin'. Make sure it ain't at your cost!'

Granger pushed through the batwing doors of the Golden Nugget into bright lights, loud voices, and the diamond-back rattle of dice. He blew air through pursed lips. The place had certainly changed since Pa had let him take his first beer. Then the Golden Nugget was no bigger than a couple of homesteader's rooms, a scattering of half-a-dozen rough tables and a plank and barrel bar. Now it could rival a place in Abilene. That is, if the cowboys were out of town on a cattle drive. The saloon was busy, but the men who sat around the tables were either deep in conver-sation or intent on their gaming. A few women sat among the men but they were quiet, clean-looking, and not show-ing too much bare flesh.

At the end of the large room on a raised platform, a group of old-timers in rusty black coats sipped from tin mugs, fiddles resting across their knees. There was space in front of them for an entertainer to sing or recite, or whatever. Over to Granger's right a pianola filled in for the music players, its notes barely audible above the hum of conversation.

By the machine, a woman, fair-haired and wearing a blue dress, stood with her back to Granger. For a moment he felt his muscles tense but the woman was too tall for Katy. He looked around the room but there was no sign of his sister's husband. Nobody paid Granger any attention as he crossed to the long mahogany bar that stretched almost the whole length of the room. The barkeep was a tall, swarthy Mexican.

'Whiskey,' Granger said.

The barkeep moved to pour from the bottle on the bar. Then a woman's voice sounded from behind Granger.

'Juan, give Mr Granger a drink from our best bottle. I'll take one, too.'

Granger turned, frowning for a moment or two as he contemplated the tall woman before him, the one he'd noticed standing by the pianola. Then his face cleared as he recognized her.

'Cora! Cora Masters! I'll be—' He stopped abruptly.

The woman smiled, showing well-cared-for teeth. 'Believe me, Matthew Granger, you were damned! Plenty of times!'

Her smile took the sting out of her words, but then her expression became sombre. 'I'm sorry about your pa, Matt. He was a good man.'

'Thanks.' She didn't flinch from his steady gaze. 'Never thought I'd see you in a saloon, Cora.'

She turned slightly to look across the large room where four men were playing cards. The one facing them, as if suddenly aware that he was being studied, looked up from his cards. Granger felt his muscles tense as he recognized John Macpherson.

'I've been with Johnny Mac for some years,' Cora said.

'An' he lets you work here?'

'Don't you damned well look at me like that, Matthew Granger! I run the books an' keep an eye out for the girls, an' that's all. Why shouldn't Johnny have me work here? He owns the place.'

Granger took a sip of his whiskey to cover his surprise. 'He's come a long way since he shot Charlie,' he said slowly.

Cora's mouth tightened. 'For God's sake, Matthew, that was fifteen years ago! Your brother was a hot-headed fool! There were ten good citizens who swore that Charlie drew first.' Her face had reddened with anger. 'If your pa hadn't sent you back East you could have ended up the same way!'

Granger remained silent, finishing his whiskey, looking over the rim of the glass directly into her eyes. As Cora's anger had suddenly welled up, so it quickly disappeared. She placed a hand on Granger's arm.

'We were young, but you could have taken me with you,' she said softly.

Granger continued to look directly into her eyes. 'Maybe I should have.'

Abruptly he looked around the saloon, and when he spoke again his voice was harsh. 'Where are Jack Daley and my sister?'

Cora pointed towards the end of the room. 'They're out back, cleaning. They were flat busted, Johnny gave them work.'

Granger put his glass on the bar. 'Thanks for the drink, Cora.'

He stepped past her, threading his way through the crowd of men standing around in small groups in front of the bar. One or two looked at him as if they recognized him but Granger ignored them. He rounded the end of the bar and pushed open the door set in the wall.

The two people working in the windowless room lit only by smoking oil lamps didn't look around as Granger stepped into the room. The woman, bent over before the deep sink, continued to scrub at greasy metal plates, while beside her a tall lean man held a large wooden tub pouring steaming water into the sink.

'Katy!' Granger said.

The woman turned, exhaustion showing in her face. Then her eyes widened as she recognized her brother. Her face crumpled, and she burst into tears, her head down. Her husband lowered the tub to the floor, standing alongside his wife, his hand on her shoulder.

'Matt, I—'

Daley's voice choked off as his wife rushed across the room to throw herself into her brother's arms, her cries a mixture of joy and despair, her tears dampening his coat. Granger wrapped his arms around her, murmuring words of consolation.

'What happened, Jack?' Granger asked finally, over Katy's shoulder.

'The bad summer two years back. Most of us homesteaders had to borrow money. The bank was good to us, and I woulda paid it off in a coupla years. Then after Pa Granger got killed Ralston made his move.'

'Why would Ralston want the homestead?'

Jack shrugged. 'Your pa kept this town goin' these past years. Ralston didn't like that. He took it out on us.'

'OK, you got much stuff in this place?'

'A few clothes, that's all.' Daley hesitated. 'Matt, we can't just leave. I'm into Macpherson for seventy dollars. Me and Katy gotta work it off.'

'Just get your stuff together.'

Gently, Granger unfolded Katy's arms from around his shoulders. He took from the pocket of his Prince Albert a snow-white handkerchief and wiped her face.

'I'll see Macpherson,' he said. He remembered something he'd seen on the ride into town. 'You know the clapboard close to the blacksmith's place? Does Sam Bryce still own it?'

'I reckon so,' Daley said. 'It's been empty since Widow Black died.'

'Get your stuff up there. Tell Sam I'll come an' talk with him.'

Without waiting for their answers, Granger turned on his heel and went back into the saloon. He threaded his way past several tables to where Macpherson and three others were playing cards. Coins and bills, bottles and glasses, were on the table in front of them.

As Granger halted, Macpherson looked up. A slow smile appeared on his fair, well-cut features. Light-coloured hair showed below his grey Stetson, and the blue sheen of an expensive Prince Albert coat covered his slim shoulders.

He put down his cards. 'Howdy, Matt. Thought I saw you talkin' to Cora. It's been a long time.' His smile widened, but his eyes were watchful. 'I hope you ain't still aimin' to shoot me.'

'Dude ain't even carryin',' said the player to Macpherson's right who wore a big Colt on his hip.

'Shut your mouth, Zack,' Macpherson said without heat. 'What can I do for you, Matt?'

'You got Jack Daley an' my sister out back workin' off seventy dollars.' Granger reached inside his jacket and took out two coins. He placed them on the table in front of Macpherson. 'They just stopped workin' here.'

One of the men at the table muttered something to the man alongside him. Macpherson looked down at the coins for a few seconds before raising his head to look around the crowded room. His eyes found the person he was searching for.

'Cora!' Macpherson called.

The woman turned away from her conversation with the Mexican barkeep and came to the table, her eyebrow

24

raised. Then she blinked rapidly a couple of times as she looked down at the table and saw the two coins.

'What we got here, Cora?' Macpherson asked.

Cora picked up one of the coins and put it between her teeth. Then she examined it, turning the coin so the lamplight shone directly onto its engraving. She put the coin on the table.

'Gold piece worth maybe thirty-six dollars, minted in California.'

Macpherson looked up slowly at Granger, before turning back to Cora.

'You sure about that?'

'I'm sure.'

The rat-featured man called Zack let out a cackle of laughter. 'Feller wants to watch hisself walkin' 'round with that sorta money in his poke.'

Granger looked down at him. 'You butt in again, an' I'm gonna take that Colt off you, an' make you eat it.'

'Why you damned—'

An outraged Zack started to rise from his chair. Macpherson grabbed his arm, forcing him back down.

'Take it easy! This ain't a place for fightin'.' He looked up at Granger.

'I'm obliged, Matt. Can't say I liked seein' Katy workin' out back.'

Granger nodded briefly and was turning away from the table when Macpherson spoke again. 'A word of advice, Matt. The town's changed since your pa sent you away on the stage all those years back. That no-good you brought in to Billy Haynes was seen rustlin' beeves off the Lazy Y a while back. Mr Ralston ain't likely to wait for Judge Parker. Last time rustlers got caught on the Lazy Y they ended up dangling from a cottonwood. You oughta make sure Billy knows that.'

CHAPTER THREE

Granger ate a good breakfast at the Chinaman's place before calling on Sam Bryce. The blacksmith's wiry hair had turned from fair to grey during Granger's absence, but the muscles still rippled in arms as thick as many men's thighs. Granger good-humouredly accepted the older man's joshing, recalling Matthew's first efforts at learning how to shoe a horse, and Sam's joking threats to take a strap to him should he not get it right next time.

'Seein' you after all this time is like havin' your pa back,' Sam said after he'd had his fun. 'Billy Haynes does his best but he's just a young feller. Ralston's lookin' to take over everythin' this side o' the river. I've knowed it a long time.' He looked hard at Granger. 'You come back to wear the badge like your pa did fer all those years?'

'No, Sam, I've business in Boston,' Granger said. 'But there is something you can do for me. You still own the clapboard where Widow Black used to be?'

Sam nodded. 'Jack Daley saw me. I told 'em they could move in.'

'You fix a rent, an' I'll settle it for a year. I'll have the money sent here to the bank. An' I'll throw in a few dollars for any tables an' chairs an' stuff.'

Sam's eyebrows shot up towards his grey hair. 'Your pa told me you was doin' well.' He held out a hand like a

26

ham. 'It's a deal.'

After leaving the smithy Granger paid a quick visit to Walter Rogers at the dry goods store. He thanked Rogers for his letter, asked after Mrs Rogers, and, as with the blacksmith, promised to return before he left town.

People were beginning to go about their business as he strolled down Main Street. Women bustled around, baskets in their hands. A drummer carrying a large bag, probably full of his samples, came out of one of the stores. Two men carrying carpentry tools were deep in conversation on the boardwalk. Granger wondered if one of them was Moses Jackson, the town's undertaker.

The air was warm, and Granger was pleased that he'd left his Prince Albert behind in his room. His grey pants were a mite too heavy, but he welcomed the freedom of wearing only a blue silk vest above his shirt. His leather armstrap would have been too conspicuous, and he'd stowed it and his knife safely away in the padlocked metal box in his room. Had he been staying around he'd have needed to buy trail clothes from Walter Rogers.

Several people greeted him on his way back to the Majestic where he intended to take coffee and smoke a cigarette before calling in at the bank. He vaguely remembered one or two of the older townsfolk but he guessed that most of them knew him only from his previous day's arrival in town. He smiled to himself. He knew he'd be forgotten once the next excitement occurred in the town.

The young man who acted as desk clerk and book-keeper called out from behind his desk as Granger entered the Majestic. In his hand the clerk held a newspaper.

'Sure sounds excitin'! You an' Mr Roberts an' them road-agents!' Puzzled by the young man's remarks, Granger walked over to the desk.

'What's all this about, Willy?'

'The town's *Reporter* got an extra three pages! Tells us all about you an' Mr Roberts fightin' off those no-goods, an' savin' decent folks!'

'Let me see that.'

Granger took the newspaper and turned to the front page. His frown deepened as he read the first lines beneath the large black headlines.

'Where's the newspaper office?' Granger barked.

'Past the sheriff's office,' Willy said, shooting nervous glances at Granger. 'Ain't you pleased the townsfolk know what you did?'

Granger put a coin on the desk. 'That's for the paper,' he snapped, and turned on his heel.

'Damn fool people,' he said aloud, going back on to Main Street, his expensive leather boots sounding on the boardwalk as he headed for the newspaper office. Unlike earlier that morning, townsfolk who greeted him received only a brief nod in return.

He passed the window, marked with the sign *Springwater Reporter* in black painted letters, and threw open the door with its cardboard sign telling the town that the newspaper was open for business.

Granger paused in the doorway, allowing his eyes to adjust from the morning sunshine behind him. Faced with an empty office, he halted at the store-styled counter behind which stood two desks, and a large wooden cabinet. Beyond them the room was taken up with the printing machinery used to produce the paper. The acrid smells of ink and paper hung in the air.

He raised his voice. 'Anybody around in this darned fool place?'

A woman appeared at the doorway at the rear of the open space. She was tall, and about the same age as

Granger. In her blue cotton dress her upper body looked strong, and she was almost pretty.

'You sound angry, Mr Granger.'

Granger was caught off balance. 'You know my name?'

She smiled. 'You're so like your father.'

'I don't know about that,' Granger said gruffly. He slapped the newspaper on to the counter. 'I'm gonna have a word with your boss about this nonsense.'

'You're speaking with the boss, as you put it,' she said. Her eyes dropped to the paper, and she nodded, her satisfaction evident. 'I've doubled my sales this week thanks to that story.'

Granger took a deep breath. 'Listen to me, ma'am! Every gun-happy fool's gonna be after me aimin' to make a reputation, you write this hogwash.'

'Gun-happy fools don't read, Mr Granger,' she said evenly. 'And Mr Morley Roberts wrote it. Although,' she added, 'it was my decision to print it.'

For a moment the name Morley Roberts meant nothing to Granger. Then he realized. 'That crazy Englishman! He's a brave son of a gun. But he writes like a fool. And you decided to print it!'

'His first attempt read like something for the *Boston Gazette*.' She laughed aloud. 'Not a style to appeal to most of my readers. Then Mr Roberts recalled a story he'd read by Ned Buntline and copied the style.'

'Then I hope you paid Roberts well. He needs the money,' Granger said, his anger fading away before this woman who appeared not the slightest bit shaken by his anger.

'I've given Mr Roberts a job and bed and board at my house,' she said. Seeing Granger's change of expression she added, 'Mr Roberts knows Latin and Greek and is a student of literature.' She smiled again. 'Those are qualities not to be found easily in Springwater, Mr Granger. I look forward to conversations with him.'

To his surprise she held out her hand. For a moment he wasn't sure how to react. Even back East where women were breaking all types of social barriers he hadn't shaken hands with a woman before.

He held out his hand, hoping she hadn't noticed his hesitation. Her hand was very slightly warm, her palm soft, but he could feel the strength in her long fingers.

'I'm Mrs Amy Morgan,' she said. 'Your father may have mentioned me in one of his letters.'

'Of course! And he talked about the newspaper.' Granger paused. 'I somehow didn't connect you with owning the *Reporter*.'

'My father started the paper almost twenty years ago.' A shadow passed across her face. 'My husband was killed during the Vicksburg Campaign and I had no children. When my father died last year I decided to stay here and continue with the paper.'

Her lips set in a firm line. 'Your father and mine set their faces against that monster Ralston taking over this town.' She blinked rapidly several times. 'And now they're both gone.'

Granger wasn't sure how to respond. He'd be foolish to say anything he'd regret. He hoped the woman wasn't thinking the same as Sam Bryce. What happened in Springwater was now no concern of his. He was satisfied that Billy had cleared up any outstanding family business. Jack and Katy would be well housed until they were back on their feet again. Ralston's takeover of the old Granger homestead stuck in his craw but, dirty move that it was, it was legal. The men who paid him good money wanted him back East. It was time he got back to work.

He was about to make a non-committal reply to Amy

Morgan's words when he was saved by the door opening behind him. He turned to see a young boy, a blue bib overall over his red shirt, a battered straw hat on his head.

'Mr Granger, sir?'

'That's me, son.'

'Sheriff Haynes needs you in the livery barn. Needs you bad, he said.'

'I'll go now. Here,' he said. Granger gave the boy a couple of coins.

'Thanks, Mr Granger!'

Granger turned to Amy Morgan. 'It's been a pleasure meeting you, Mrs Morgan.'

'Perhaps you'd come for supper before you leave town, Mr Granger.'

'I'd like that, Mrs Morgan.' He touched the brim of his Dakota, his face broadening with a smile. 'I hope I can keep up with the conversation.'

Granger found the livery twenty yards from the newspaper office at the entrance to the next alley on Main Street. The large double doors fronting the street were closed and Granger stepped off the boards to cross the alleyway to the side door. The door seemed to be permanently left unbarred, as it swung back at his touch. He ducked his head and stepped into the shadowy barn. The bitter tang of horses confined in small spaces came to his nostrils. As Granger closed the door behind him the animals stirred in their stalls, aware of his presence, hoofs rustling in the straw. A piebald over to Granger's left slurped noisily at a water trough. There was no sign of Wilkins, the livery owner.

'Billy!' Granger called.

Something hard and solid smashed against the side of his head, and his knees buckled. A heavy boot crashed against his spine, and he tottered forward a few paces and fell forward, a sharp pain flashing across his nose as he fell face down in the thin covering of straw above the hard-packed dirt. Another boot smashed down on his arm, and amongst the black clouds that swirled around his head he heard a voice snarl.

'He ain't carryin' his knife!'

Hands grabbed his arms, and hauled him upright, supporting his sagging body on either side. He held himself deliberately slack. There was no sense in these no-goods knowing he could still think straight. His head began to clear faster, the black clouds drifting away like smoke in the wind. The side of his head and his nose hurt like hell, but he knew the blow hadn't been meant to kill him or knock him unconscious. What did the owl hoots want from him? Was it information or were they delivering a message? He raised his head more slowly than he needed to.

In front of Granger, two more men stood, their heads covered with linen bags, holes cut to show their eyes and mouths. Summoning up all his remaining strength Granger lashed out at the men with both his boots off the ground. His efforts were wasted, his boots flailing short of their target as the men jumped aside, and those gripping his arms dragged him back.

'Goddamn you, Granger!' the taller of the two men shouted. 'We jest know you're gonna try an' poke that nose o' yourn in other folk's business. So we're here to tell you what you're gonna do.'

Through a split in the linen bag Granger could see the man's mouth pull back, showing misshapen brown teeth.

'You're gonna get back on the stage to Cheyenne an' go back to your fancy friends in Boston. Stick to the bankin' business, Granger. We don't wanna see your hide 'round these parts.'

'An' if I don't wanna go?' Granger struggled to get out the words.

The tall man's bunched fist smashed into Granger's stomach. Air rushed from his body, and, as his captors released their holds, he sank to the straw desperately trying to suck in air.

All four fell on him. Their boots lashed into his body, the men moving along the barn as Granger rolled along the ground vainly tried to avoid their kicks, trying to regain his feet. He managed to get a knee on to the ground for leverage but a boot into his ribs sent him face down once more. He pulled up his knees, his chin on his chest, attempting to protect his head with curled arms. Boots and fists rained on him. He clenched his eyes shut, willing himself not to cry out. Through the red streaks of pain he heard them curse.

'Get on that goddamn stage, Granger! Next time we'll kill you!'

Black clouds swirled to cover the red streaks that exploded in his brain and, with a sense of blessed relief, he knew no more.

CHAPTER FOUR

Both Amy Morgan and Morley Roberts looked up from the table as Matt Granger entered the dining-room of the large house. They exchanged glances as Granger closed the door.

Roberts stood up. 'Good to see you back on your feet, Mr Granger. You gave us all a worrying time these last three weeks.'

'Thank you, Mr Roberts,' Granger said. 'I'm obliged to you, Mrs Morgan, for your hospitality.' He gave a short bow in her direction, trying not to wince as a spasm of pain flickered in the small of his back.

'You have a gentle manner, Mr Granger, but I think not too many bows for a while,' she said, sympathy showing in the curve of her full lips.

'Your presence has been welcome. You've saved my reputation with Springwater's ladies!'

She laughed aloud, and Granger wondered if she had any idea how much he liked to hear that. 'Mr Roberts in the house was a cause for gossip,' she went on. 'Two gentlemen, with one injured, and they see me as an angel of mercy!'

'Doc Simmons is a good man, knows his job,' Granger said.

'He was one of the few men to stand with your father and mine,' she said. She shook her head slightly as if to banish sad thoughts, and picked up a tiny hand-bell.

'Are you able to eat anything, Mr Granger?'

Granger looked down at the rough pants and shirt Roberts had found for him from a box in a storeroom of Amy Morgan's. After the slop he'd been eating for the last couple of weeks he was burning to get some real meat inside him.

'You mind me comin' to the table like this?'

For an answer she rang the hand-bell and when the door to the dining-room opened she addressed the young girl who wore a white apron over a blue cotton dress and a small white cap over her dark hair.

'Rosa, bring Mr Granger some supper.' She glanced at Granger taking his seat alongside Roberts. 'I think you'd better make that a very large steak!'

'Yes, mum,' Rosa said, with a little bobbed curtsey. She appeared to take a deep breath as she looked towards Granger. 'Mr Matt, me an' Polly and Hetty jest wanna say how happy we are to see you up an' about agin.'

Her face turned a deep red, and before Granger could reply she had stepped back and closed the door. Granger looked at both Amy Morgan and Roberts in turn, seeing on their faces expressions of amusement at his discomfort.

'Don't you both go putting this in the *Reporter*!'

'When men write for profit,' said Roberts, 'they are not very delicate.'

'Enough of your quotations, Mr Roberts!' Amy said. 'We must allow Mr Granger to eat his supper. If he's to undertake the long journey back East then he needs to be well again.'

Granger looked at her sharply. 'You've got it wrong, Mrs Morgan. I'm not goin' anyplace. Aside from back to the Majestic, I mean.'

Amy Morgan's eyes shone with pleasure. 'Don't ruin my reputation again, Mr Granger,' she said with mock-seriousness. 'You're welcome to stay here.' She raised her delicate eyebrows. 'But what have you in mind?'

'I'm well enough now an' I've been a lot worse in the past. I don't know who those no-goods were in the livery. The stage hold-up gang, mebbe, or that trail-trash I saw around Macpherson. Whoever they were, I'm gonna call their bluff an' find out what's goin' on in this town.'

Again Amy Morgan raised her eyebrows. 'We know what's going on, Mr Granger. Ralston is trying to take over Springwater.'

Granger nodded. 'But why? It makes no sense. He's got thousands of acres across the river. What's he aimin' for on this side? What makes my family's old homestead so important to him that he has to drive out Jack and Katy as soon as my pa was killed? Take my word, Ralston does nothing without some aim in mind.'

'I was riding by your family's old place last week,' Roberts said. 'The river's shallow enough there for Ralston to bring across his cattle.'

'It's the only place for cattle to ford the river for several miles north or south,' Amy Morgan said. 'But Ralston would gain nothing from that. The railhead is to the south-west of the Lazy Y. Ralston's cowboys started out with the herd last week.'

'How long they likely to be away?' Granger asked.

'Forty days, at least,' Amy Morgan said. 'Ralston stays at the ranch, surrounded by those gunslingers of his.'

'I'm gonna begin pokin' 'round tomorrow,' Granger said. 'After I've seen Walter Rogers, an' bought a few things, I'm gonna find out why the bank sold Jack's debt to Ralston.' He looked towards the doorway as Rosa knocked and entered the room carrying before her a large steaming plate.

'An' that chunk o' beef will sure have me ready to roll!'

From behind the counter of the dry goods store Walter Rogers gave a cry of pleasure as Granger stepped in from the early morning sun shining down on Main Street.

'Matt! Thought you'd left town without me gettin' a chance to see you again! I heard you'd been stayin' at the Morgan place.' Rogers stopped abruptly and peered across the counter to examine the side of Granger's face. 'Oh, lordy! What you been up to?'

'Lyin' low, Mr Rogers. But I'm up an' about now, an' I need trail clothes.'

'I ain't askin' why! Guess it's none o' my business. Jest like your pa!' Rogers cast an appraising eye over the rough shirt and pants worn by Granger, mentally measuring him for size. For a moment his gaze lingered over the tooled leather gunbelt and the Navy Colt on Granger's hip.

'What happened to the fancy clothes you was wearin' last time?'

'It's a long story, Mr Rogers.'

Rogers waited, but seeing that Granger was not going to explain further, the store-keeper looked through the window overlooking Main Street. Outside, a horse stood quietly. In the absence of the mount's saddle and bridle a rough length of rope had been turned around the animal's head and secured to the hitching rail.

'That your palomino, Matt? Looks a good 'un.'

'Horse is fine, I struck lucky with the livery,' Granger said. That wasn't the smartest thought of his day, he suddenly realized, but he brushed it away. 'I'll need a rig, you got somethin' I like.'

'OK, but pants and shirts first,' Rogers said. A shadow suddenly passed across his face, as he took stuff down from a shelf. 'Still seems mighty strange me not expectin' your pa in for coffee an' a smoke.'

'What the hell sent Pa rushin' out to the bank like that?'

Rogers frowned as he recalled the events of a few weeks before. 'We was both sittin' 'round the stove, same as always.

Talkin' about Billy's ma, if I remember right. Then there was this shot we both heard from 'cross the street. Your pa jumped to his feet, pullin' out that big Peacemaker o' his, and ran out. He got one of the damned villains afore one got him. I saw it all from that window over there.'

'Hold on there. Didn't Pa get all three of 'em?'

Rogers shook his head. 'Macpherson, feller who owns the saloon, got the other two. Came 'round the corner as if on a Sunday stroll. Saw what was happenin' an' drew his gun.' Rogers sucked in air. 'You know he's as fast as he ever was. He took them other two out afore they made their hosses.'

Rogers shook his head as if wanting to forget the whole incident. He shot a glance at Granger's Dakota, the only item not ruined by blood in the encounter with the four no-goods in the livery.

'That's a fine hat you got there, Matt. Got a Stetson here, worth five dollars. Care to exchange?'

Granger didn't reply immediately, his thoughts racing. Why the hell hadn't Billy mentioned Macpherson's involvement? Then he remembered his own anger, cutting off Billy's words, when he asked why Jenkins wasn't around. Later in the saloon had Macpherson deliberately avoided mentioning his own involvement? Time was, Macpherson would have been strutting around town telling folks how good he was with a sidearm and what a brave fellow he was to take on the outlaws.

'Sure, why not,' Granger answered Rogers finally.

He reached up and took off his Dakota. It had cost him seven fifty in some fancy place down in Cheyenne. Damned hat was far too fancy for Springwater, and for what he hoped to be doing these next few days. He looked over to the corner of the large store where a number of saddles were lined up on a wooden horse.

'I'll take a look at those.'

Rogers came from behind the counter, and joined Granger who was running his fingers over the smooth leather of the first saddle.

'You wanna try somethin' different?' Rogers asked. 'I can recommend this. Probably the best saddle I've ever stocked. Feller by the name of Frank Meanea, down in Cheyenne, brought this out in '70.'

Granger looked down at the saddle drawn to his attention. Unusually, a leather flange extended to the rear of the cantle.

'I'll take it.' Granger looked up to the shelves where boxes of ammunition were neatly stacked in rows. 'An' a coupla boxes of thirty-six.'

He looked around again at the shelves piled high with clothing. 'An Englishman by the name of Roberts is gonna come callin'. Give him a coupla pairs o' pants an' a coupla shirts. I'm good for 'em.' He looked into a corner of the store. 'An' find him a trail jacket. One with a big pocket up here.' Granger put his hand to his chest. 'Feller likes to carry a book with him.'

'That's mighty generous of you, Matt.'

'Roberts saved my life the day those no-goods attacked the stage. Then he came lookin' for me in the livery when I got bushwhacked. Found me an' Wilkins down on our faces.' Granger shrugged 'Roberts is flat broke. I guess I owe him somethin'.'

'I'll make sure that's done.' Rogers hesitated, looking thoughtfully at Granger. 'Matt, me an' your pa were friends for many years,' he said slowly. 'I knew your ma and Billy's. I remember Charlie well, an' I've known you since you were in britches an' stockin's.'

The storekeeper's eyes were shadowed, and Granger guessed that his own transformation from Boston gentleman to something very different was troubling Rogers.

'Matt, you Grangers are all alike. An' when your pa was sheriff the whole town was mighty glad of it. If he an' Caleb White at the *Reporter* hadn't stood up strong, Ralston'd be ownin' this town now, an' every man doin' exactly what Ralston ordered. Billy's doin' his best to follow your pa, even if Ralston did fix his badge. Maybe Ralston made a mistake doin' that. Anyways, I don't know what you're plannin' but I got a bad feelin'. I hope to tarnation you ain't gonna start a war.'

'I don't plan on startin' a war, Mr Rogers. But if Ralston does, I'm gonna be 'round to finish it.'

Granger waited until the bank was about to close for the midday meal before making his play. He stood a foot inside the door waiting until the teller had left before following Henry Fells behind the counter and taking the proffered chair in front of the banker's desk.

Granger studied the banker's ashen face as Fells fumbled for papers with shaking hands. The banker looked as if he'd become a man who wasn't slow to draw a cork. What the hell had happened to him? His eyes were clouded and his face had an unhealthy sheen. Granger remembered Fells as an upright, cheerful man, a churchgoer, always willing to give others a helping hand when needed.

'Was Jack Daley the only homesteader you had paper on?' Granger asked.

Fells raised his head, averting his eyes when meeting Granger's hard stare. 'I'm not sure I can tell you—'

Granger cut in, his voice harsh. 'Mr Fells, I remember you an' Pa were good friends. Pa was hardly cold in his grave when Ralston moved in and took over the Granger place. I ain't leavin' this bank until you tell me how and why he did that.'

Fells's mouth tightened. His gaze was still over

40

Granger's shoulder, as if the banker was physically unable to maintain any eye contact.

'Lots of folks have had their troubles,' Fells said slowly.

'I know that,' Granger said, his voice quieter. 'I'm not looking for you to break any promises to folks 'round here. But Ralston's aimin' for somethin', and takin' over the Granger homestead is part of what he's doin'.'

Fells sat straighter in his chair, as if attempting to summon the man he once was. 'It was that damned winter three years ago,' he said. 'Nobody could make a cent. Lots of folks in the town, homesteaders around these parts, I managed to get money from Cheyenne to see them through.'

Granger frowned. 'Have most of 'em bought back their paper?'

Fells shook his head. 'No,' he said, his voice low.

'You sell any others to Ralston?'

Fells's head was almost down on his chest. 'No.'

'So why sell Jack's paper?'

Fells lifted his head, the expression in his eyes appearing to plead for Granger's understanding. 'I swear I didn't know he'd turn out Jack Daley. Why would he do something like that?'

'Answer the question, Mr Fells. Why did you sell Jack's paper?'

Fells's head was down again. 'I'd lent too much money out, and Ralston must have heard I was going to be fired. I'm too old to start again and God knows what would have happened to us. Ralston came in here and said he'd deposit fifty thousand dollars in Cheyenne and tell my people there that I'd arranged it. He knew that would make my position safe. In exchange I was to sell him Jack Daley's paper.'

For fully thirty seconds Granger gazed at the banker

across the paper-littered desk. He guessed that as soon as he was out of the door Fells would reach for the drawer in his desk towards which the banker's eyes had been shifting every few moments. But whiskey wasn't going to drown the banker's conscience, nor hide the anguish in the man's eyes. In his time Granger had seen plenty of guilty men. Most of them got what they deserved, either at the end of a rope or locked away in a cage. Unless he was mistaken Fells didn't deserve what he was going through. Damn Ralston to hell! How many more men had the rancher broken in the last fifteen years?

Granger stood up from his chair. 'I'm obliged to you, Mr Fells. Ralston had you plumb in his sights, I can see that.' His mouth tightened. 'You're not the first, maybe you'll be one of the last.'

His gaze shifted to the clock pinned to the wall a few feet above the man's head. A small hole with ragged metal edges showed in the face to the left of the two black hands.

'The hold-up men who killed my pa did that?' Granger asked.

Fells turned in his chair to look up. 'I thought my time had come, Mr Granger. They'd already got the money and the leader aimed his pistol straight at me. Then the one with a scatter-gun said they were running out of time. And the man raised his pistol and fired at the clock.'

'That's damned strange.'

Fells nodded. 'I've been meaning to ask Billy Haynes what he could make of it.' The banker shrugged. 'Too late for that now, I guess.'

Granger looked sharply at the banker. 'What do you mean by that, Mr Fells?'

The banker stood up from his chair. 'Haven't you heard? Billy Haynes rode out of town last night. I heard he told folks he wasn't coming back.'

CHAPTER FIVE

Granger pushed open the door to the sheriff's office. After his eyes had adjusted to the shadowy room he saw that nothing had changed, save for the man behind the desk lolling in the high-backed chair tilted against the whitewashed wall. As Granger closed the door John Macpherson pushed the chair forward to the floor and swung his boots down from the desk.

'Howdy, Matt.' Macpherson said. 'Thought at first you'd gone back to Boston. Then I heard you'd moved in with that fancy Amy Morgan.' A smile broadened his face as he stared deliberately at the bruises on the side of Granger's face. 'She getting rough with you, Matt? Lot of menfolk 'round town going to be real jealous.'

'You got the wrong idea,' Granger said. 'Where's Billy?'

'Don't rightly know. I'm told he quit town last night.' Macpherson said. He took a short cigar from a box on the desk. 'You fancy one of these?'

Granger shook his head. 'Billy ain't a quitter,' he said.

Macpherson lit his cigar with a match taken from his vest pocket. 'So you say,' he said. 'But he ain't here now, Matt.'

He tilted his chair again, and leaned back against the wall. 'If you're looking to wear the badge, you're too late. Folks in town have decided I'm their man.' He reached

43

forward to the desk and picked up the shiny metal star. 'There'll have to be an election, the town council tell me.' He held the badge against his shirt. 'Maybe you could stand against me.'

'You givin' up runnin' the saloon?'

Macpherson shrugged. 'Cora's been doing that for years. She's smarter with the figures than I ever was. Even Mr Ralston thinks highly of her. I'm just gonna count the profits, and see the town gets some decent law.'

'You're talkin' Ralston's law.'

'Means the same around here, Matt. You should know that.'

Macpherson swung his boots on to the desk again, blue smoke curled up above his head. 'Go back East, Matt. I see you in trail clothes, that Navy Colt on your hip I wonder what you're trying to prove. You, me, Cora, we ain't brats in your ma's schoolroom any more. Forget Springwater, this town don't concern you no more. I know you're never going to forget I shot Charlie. If things could have been different I'd have made them so. But all that happened a long time ago, and it was him or me.'

'Same as that hold-up gang at the bank,' Granger said.

'Yeah, that's about right, Matt. Maybe had I done better I could have saved your pa.'

Granger turned on his heel, and opened the door, allowing sunlight to flood into the office. In the doorway he turned back to Macpherson.

'Johnny Mac,' he said, 'you were a lyin' sonovabitch when you wore leather britches: I guess you ain't changed none.'

Granger stepped out into the street and closed the door quietly behind him.

Two townsmen driving a buggy came through the high,

wide entrance to the livery stable as Granger stepped down from the boardwalk and reached the hardpack of the alleyway. Both men nodded a greeting, and they were several yards past him when Granger overheard the passenger's words to his companion.

'I'd sure like that Granger feller to follow his pa,' he said. 'Billy Haynes was doing his best but he never stood a chance.'

Was that said deliberately so he could hear? Granger's mouth tightened, his teeth worrying his lip. Damn town! If he had any sense he'd take the stage back to Cheyenne as soon as he could. Maybe Macpherson had a point. What was he trying to prove? That Ralston couldn't railroad the Grangers? That he'd pay one day for Charlie's death? Sure, Macpherson pulled the trigger, but Ralston set it up, Granger was sure. Charlie and Ralston's daughter were planning to hightail it out of town together, beyond her father's reach. Ralston got to hear of it and solved the problem his own way. With the older Granger dead, maybe Ralston had reckoned he'd control young Billy when he fixed the badge for him. Maybe Billy couldn't stomach the set-up anymore.

Granger stepped through the doorway into the barn, his glance shifting to the spot in the middle of the barn where he'd taken a beating. The marks on his body were fading but the scars on his pride had been with him these last three weeks. In that comfortable bed in the house of Amy Morgan he'd turned over the incident in his mind a hundred times. The stagecoach *bandidos*, if that's who his attackers were, could have easily guessed that he was from back East. But the tallest one had told him to get back to his banking friends. How would a road-agent know something like that?

A tall skinny man in dusty blue coveralls appeared from

out of an empty stall. He stepped the few paces towards the entrance, his left leg dragging as if he'd been badly kicked by a horse at some time.

'Howdy, Mr Granger. You here for your palomino?

'You fixed the plates yet, Mr Wilkins?'

'Sure have. Hoss needed four new ones, like I told you.'

'So you did.' He looked carefully at the livery owner. 'You OK now?'

'I've been fine, Mr Granger. But I'm sure glad that Englishman came 'round when he did.' He shrugged. 'Those no-goods didn't hit me too hard.'

A thought came to Granger. 'You here last night when Billy Haynes came for his horse?'

'Yeah, I was finishin' up for the night. But Billy didn't come hisself. He sent some other feller.'

'Is that so? You seen this feller before?'

Wilkins shook his head. 'A stranger to me, but he sure was ornery. I told him the sheriff's roan had a broken plate, an' I was gonna fix it.'

'So just what did this feller say?'

'Tol' me to fergit it. Sheriff had more to think about than a broken plate.'

Granger thought for a moment. 'What sorta mark this broken plate make?'

Wilkins reached behind to pick up a long-handled fork. With the edge of his boot he brushed away the straw at his feet. Using the sharp point of one of the tines he drew a pattern on the dirt floor.

'Like that, Mr Granger. Right foreleg, with a break on the inside edge.'

Granger nodded. 'Thanks, Mr Wilkins. I'll settle with you when I get back.'

Ten minutes later Granger trotted his palomino along Main Street heading out of town. Macpherson was talking with someone in front of the sheriff's office, and they turned his way as he passed them. There was a snicker of laughter and for a moment he was tempted to turn back. To hell with it! Catching up with Billy was likely to take some hard riding and he didn't want to waste time.

At the end of the street he left the hardpack and joined the rough ground of the trail. Reckoning that Billy would head for Cheyenne, Granger rode for a further mile before taking the fork that headed south. Even if proved wrong he reckoned he'd have time to turn back and take the trail east. Billy wouldn't travel too far by night, and the broken plate on his roan might slow him down some.

Moving along the trail at a trot, Granger kept his head down, searching the rough ground of the trail. The wheels of the stage had cut sharp furrows in the ground since the fall of rain a few days before. The soil was soft enough to show where the six horses hauling the stage had trod. In some places, where the ground had already been holding water, their tracks were maybe two or three inches deep.

Two miles down the trail he thought he'd picked up the trail but his grunt of triumph was stifled as he realized his mistake. Would he have to turn back? Billy could have ridden east after all. He'd heard talk about a ranch in that direction which was twice as large as Ralston's place. Maybe Billy was going there looking for work before moving on. He decided to give it another mile and if he couldn't pick up the trail he'd go back. Head down, his eyes moving to and fro, he held the palomino in a trot.

At the moment when he was telling himself that it was time to turn back Granger thought he spotted the mark of the roan's broken plate. He halted his horse and slid from the saddle, more cautious this time. He squatted down, letting go of the reins, allowing the palomino to nibble at the bunch and buffalo grass at the side of the trail.

'That's Billy!' Granger said aloud.

He stood up and walked a few yards along the trail. Sure enough, again the pattern showed in the soil. Though it was just possible Billy had previously ridden along here with a broken plate it was unlikely. He realized he could be in for a long ride, depending on how long Billy had ridden during the night. Maybe knowing the trail, Billy would have pushed along, anxious to put space between himself and Springwater.

That's what he was finding so damned puzzling. Billy wasn't a quitter, he was sure. He didn't know the young man well, but in a rare letter his father had once praised Billy's courage when they'd both been out hunting. Maybe there was something going on with Billy he hadn't yet got a handle on.

Granger walked back to his palomino, unbuckled his saddle-bag and pulled out his water bottle and a cotton bag. Cold water and jerky was a poor meal after the food at Amy Morgan's place. He smiled to himself. Maybe he shouldn't get too comfortable sharing her table. He had a job to do back East, and getting involved with a strong-willed woman was not a smart move. He took a pull from the water bottle, and bit off a chunk of the dried meat. Damned jerky was as dry and tough as ever. He took another gulp of the water. Then a voice rang out.

'Hold it right there, mister! You move an inch an' I'll gun you down!'

His water bottle still held halfway from his mouth, Granger looked in the direction from which the warning had been shouted. A stand of cottonwoods stood at the top of a long slope maybe fifty yards over to his left. Between the closely grown trees he could make out the shape of a horse. To its right, partly concealed, stood a man, his long gun showing darkly against the trunk of the tree.

'Billy Haynes!' Granger shouted. 'Is that you?'

There was a pause. Then the man stepped from behind the cottonwood. 'Matt? What the hell you doin' here?'

'That's what I'm gonna ask you! C'mon, let's get a fire goin'. I sure need some coffee!'

Ten minutes later, in a small clearing on the edge of the cottonwoods furthest away from the trail, Billy poured coffee into Granger's proffered tin cup.

'OK, Billy. Tell me what happened.'

Haynes leaned his back against a tree, and took a sip of his coffee, appearing to get his thoughts in order. 'I was doin' my rounds. Same routine I've followed since I took on the job. I was in the alleyway down by the dry goods store when four men jumped me.'

'Your sidearm on your belt?'

Haynes's face went pink. 'We ain't had trouble in town for a long time.'

'Next time you carry a scatter-gun.'

Billy looked at Granger. 'You reckon there's gonna be a next time?'

'Go on tellin' me what happened.'

'They took my old Colt an' we went back to the office. That's when I saw they'd got these bags over their heads, with holes cut for their eyes and mouths. I got no idea who they were. They mighta been Celestials for all I could tell.'

'What happened then?'

'They tol' me to get my stuff together, an' one of 'em left. Then they gave me a choice. Ride outa town an' keep goin'. They'd shoot me down if I ever set foot in Springwater agin.'

'An' you said you'd keep ridin'.'

Haynes's shoulders lifted a fraction. 'If I hadn't agreed

they were gonna ride with me an' shoot me when we got clear of town. They let me keep my long gun and sidearm, but they emptied 'em both.'

Granger frowned. 'What about the long gun you used back there?'

'I was bluffin'. Damn piece is empty.'

Granger grinned. 'You crazy sonovabitch! Pa woulda been proud of you.' His grin faded. 'So what you plannin' now?'

Haynes shrugged himself up against the trunk of the tree, a determined look on his face. 'I'm goin' back. Somebody's gotta make sure there's law in Springwater. I been takin' the money, so I guess it's gonna have to be me.'

'Macpherson's tryin' to take over the badge.'

Haynes's fingers brushed the badge that was still pinned to his shirt, and Granger realized that Macpherson must have found a spare one.

'I'm the duly elected sheriff of Springwater, an' I hold the badge until I decide to quit. Macpherson's gonna have to be told that.' He pursed his lips, blowing out air. 'I know he's damned fast, but I gotta try or I'm gonna be runnin' away all my life.'

Granger threw the last of his coffee into the flames of the fire, and stood up. 'I gotta Colt Navy in my saddle-bag. You reckon you can handle that?'

Haynes nodded. 'Sure.'

'You get yourself one when we get back. You shoot a man you wanna make sure he ain't gonna shoot back.' Granger paused. 'You're gonna need a deputy for a while. You got a Bible with you?'

'I can swear you in, all legal. But I ain't got a deputy's badge.'

'You let me take care o' that.' Granger's hand brushed

the butt of his Navy. 'We'll set off at first light. Then we'll go call on Johnny Mac.'

CHAPTER SIX

They were about half a mile from Springwater when Granger saw the buggy appear from around the curve of the trail. His hand moved towards the butt of his Navy but he relaxed when he saw the single figure was a woman.

For a moment he thought it might be Amy Morgan, but as he and Billy drew closer he could see that it was Cora driving the Appaloosa. Below a dark-blue hat her hair was up in some sort of knot he'd seen on women back in Boston. Above a blue skirt she wore a short plum-coloured jacket which opened near the neck to show a creamy silk shirt pinned at her throat with a blood-red brooch.

'Sure is a fine-looking woman,' Billy said. 'Where d'you reckon she's goin' headin' this way?'

They both reined in to a trot as they closed on the buggy, Cora leaning back on the reins of the Appaloosa as both men brought their mounts to a halt. Granger touched a finger to the brim of his Stetson. He saw her eyes were red-rimmed as if she'd been crying or was maybe short of sleep.

'Howdy Cora,' he said. 'Sure is a fine day for a drive.'

Colour rose to Cora's face, save for twin spots of white on her high cheekbones. 'Don't you goddamn sweet-talk me, Matthew Granger! I've been up all night waitin' for

you to ride in! I know what you and Billy are plannin'.'
Her eyes flashed to and fro between Granger and Billy.
'What is it with you men that you gotta go killin' each
other?'

'Now hold on, Miss Cora,' Billy said. 'We ain't aimin' to
kill anyone. I'm just goin' back to my office, that's all.'

'You quit two nights ago, Billy Haynes! The whole
town's talkin' about it. Why in tarnation don't you stay
quit?' Cora snapped.

'I got a job to do, Miss Cora,' Billy said firmly. 'The
town's been payin' me these last weeks, an' I don't aim to
let folks down.'

'For God's sake, Billy! You get yourself killed, folks here
won't give spit on a rock!'

'That's as maybe, ma'am, but I'm still goin' back.'

'Billy didn't quit,' Granger said. 'He was forced outa
town by four gunslingers. I know it, you know it, an'
Johnny Mac knows it.'

'An' I s'pose you're gonna make things right again?'
Cora snapped.

'No. Billy's gonna do that. I'm just along to lend a
hand.'

Cora shook her head in frustration. 'I told Johnny Mac
you'd be back with Billy but he wouldn't listen.' Her eyes
implored him to listen to her. 'Please, Matt, I don't want
you and Johnny fighting. You'll get yourself killed, or
you'll kill him, I know it.'

'You heard Billy. We ain't aimin' to kill anyone.' His
mouth pulled back in a wry smile. 'An' I sure ain't meanin'
to get killed.'

Cora looked at each of the men in turn, opening her
mouth with the apparent intention of pleading with them
again, then seeing their set expressions, her mouth closed
sharply, her face again tightening with anger.

'Damn you Grangers! You've given me nothing but heartache!'

She tugged violently at the reins, the Appaloosa stamping a foreleg on the rough ground before turning its head to start the buggy moving. Cora swung around in the buggy seat to shout at Granger.

'You're just lookin' to settle accounts for your brother! That's what this is all about!'

With a toss of her head and a flick of the Appaloosa's reins Cora headed back towards the town watched by the two men. When she was fifty yards away from them down the trail Billy broke the silence.

'Has Cora got it right, Matt? Is this all about Charlie?'

Granger waited a few seconds before replying. 'Charlie might have somethin' to do with it, but Pa gave his life for this town. I ain't walkin' away from that.' He turned back from Billy to look towards the town.

'They'll be waitin' for us, Billy.'

'You reckon they'll bushwack us?'

Granger shook his head. 'Macpherson's ornery but he ain't a backshooter.' He touched his spurs to the palomino's sides. 'Johnny Mac reckons he's fast enough not to need that.'

'I see 'em,' said Billy. 'In front of my office.'

Granger and Billy, horses abreast of each other, halted at the spot where the rough ground of the trail gave place to the hardpack of Main Street. The early morning sun behind Granger's shoulder threw their shadows on the ground. If shooting broke out, the light was where he wanted it.

The street was unusually quiet for the time of the day. Instead of the bustle Granger had observed when he first rode into town there were few townspeople around. There

54

were no women, Granger noticed. Two old-timers crossing the street looked their way and quickened their pace to mount the steps in front of the Chinaman's place. It looked like the whole town knew Billy was coming back.

In front of the sheriff's office, at the bottom of the steps leading down from the boardwalk two men stared in their direction. Macpherson stood with his hands on his belt. The man alongside him, Zack from the saloon, Granger realized, stood with his hands held loosely by his side.

As Granger and Billy nudged their mounts forward into a walk, the two men shifted to stand away from the board-walk steps. Granger saw Macpherson turn his head briefly to look behind him. Another gun hidden in an alleyway? No, that wasn't Macpherson's style. More likely he was checking that no townsman was in the line of fire. A new sheriff wouldn't want dead townsfolk on his account.

'I'll watch Johnny Mac,' Granger said. 'You keep your eyes on that critter Zack. An' don't take 'em off him before I say so.'

'They're both fast, ain't they, Matt?'

Granger turned his head to look directly at his step-brother. 'You listen real good, Billy. We want to live another day, an' we're gonna take it nice an' easy. You're the lawfully elected sheriff o' Springwater. We gotta aim to remind 'em of that. But if shootin' starts, you blast away with everythin' you got. Just remember what I tol' you about watchin' Zack.'

'Sure, Matt.'

Granger remained staring hard at Billy. There was a set about the young man's mouth which reminded him of Pa. It couldn't be Granger blood, Billy was two years old when Pa had married Billy's mother. But then again, maybe it was blood. Billy's father had died charging Johnny Rebs' guns at Wilderness. Haynes must have known what was likely to happen, and that took more courage than most men had. Maybe that's what was showing on Billy's face. Satisfied, Granger urged his mount into a trot.

'Let's go get that badge, Billy,' he said.

'Howdy, Matt,' Macpherson said easily, as Granger and Billy stepped down from their horses. Granger kept his eyes on the two men as Billy secured both their horses to the hitching rail.

'This could get you into a heap of trouble, Johnny Mac,' Granger said.

Macpherson didn't answer him, watching Billy move alongside Granger, a little too close. A half-smile appeared as he saw Granger shift a pace.

'Folks reckoned you'd quit when you left town, Billy,' Macpherson said. 'Guess I'm gonna be wearin' the badge from now on.'

'I ain't left town, Mr Macpherson,' Billy answered, although his eyes were on Zack. 'An' I'm the elected sheriff of Springwater. What you're tryin' is against the law, an' Judge Parker will back me. You take off that badge or I'm gonna have to take you into my lawful custody.'

Zack snickered. 'You hear that, Mr Macpherson? Young Billy's gonna put you in jail. Maybe he reckons the dude's gonna help him.' He snickered again. 'I sure hate to pass up the chance o' bein' deputy.'

'There's only one sworn deputy in this town an' that's Mr Granger,' Billy said, his eyes not moving from Zack's gunhand.

'Is that what you got on your shirt, Matt? Fancy kinda badge for a Springwater deputy,' Macpherson said.

Granger stood quite still, his hand loose at his side. 'You heard what Billy said. It's your play, Johnny Mac,' Granger said.

'An' s'posin' I don't fold?' The half-smile on Macpherson's face was stiffening. 'S'posin' I raise you.'

'Billy's gonna put you in jail waitin' for Judge Parker. The judge don't get here for a month so Billy tells me.'

'An you're gonna help Billy?'

'I'm gonna help him,' Granger said evenly.

Macpherson appeared to turn over his options in his mind. His hands shifted an inch or two on his belt. 'You faster with that Navy than you used to be?'

'I guess there's only one way to find out,' Granger said quietly. 'You really lookin' fer that, Johnny Mac?'

All four men shifted slightly, each aware that Macpherson's answer would decide the outcome of the confrontation. Granger was surprised to see Macpherson's stare shift a fraction to look beyond him along Main Street. Was he looking towards the saloon? Was Cora a witness to what was going on in front of the sheriff's office?

Macpherson again shifted his gaze to look directly at Granger. His gunhand moved, but slowly, reaching up to unpin the badge from his shirt. He tossed it the few feet on to the steps where it fell with a metallic ring. If Macpherson had been trying to shift Granger's attention from his gunhand he hadn't succeeded.

'Guess I don't get to be sheriff this year,' Macpherson said.

'Then it's over,' Billy said.

Billy turned away towards the steps, and Zack's hand moved an inch from his side. Granger's Navy came out of its holster with one smooth motion, evidence of much practice, and he sideswiped Zack's chin with the barrel. There was a grunt of pain and the would-be deputy, his sidearm half out of its holster, dropped like a sack of corn to the hardpack.

Billy, his mouth open, stood frozen with one foot on the

bottom step leading up to his office. Macpherson hadn't moved, his eyes on Granger as if calculating his next move. Then he looked down at the unconscious man.

'Zack Rudman woulda made a lousy deputy,' he said. 'Too hot-headed, I guess.' He looked up at Granger. 'You're faster than in the old days,' he said. 'Maybe even as fast as me.'

'Let's hope we don't have to find out, Johnny Mac,' Granger said. 'You wanna get this trail-trash shifted?'

Amy Morgan and Morley Roberts, behind their desks in the office of the *Reporter*, were hanging on every word spoken by Granger as he paced up and down recounting events from the time he'd ridden out of town to look for Billy Haynes. Roberts was scribbling furiously in his leather-backed notebook.

Granger paused with his account and looked at the Englishman. 'I thought you'd finished with that book.'

Roberts looked up with a grin. 'A printer in New York gave me a boxful in exchange for a few days' work.' He looked down at his notes. 'So what happened then?' he asked.

'Two fellers came out of the saloon and dragged Zack away while Johnny Mac walked back down Main Street as if he'd just walked out of church. Billy's got his badge back, an' the town's councilmen have given him their support.'

'What happened to that road-agent we brought in?' Roberts asked.

'Disappeared. Those four no-goods who chased Billy outa town musta broke him out. Johnny Mac wouldn't risk doin' that. Word got down to Cheyenne he's bustin' out prisoners an' he'd have a US Marshal after him.'

'Do you think Ralston was behind all this? Were they his

men who forced Billy out?' Amy asked.

'Who else? I reckon Billy was beginnin' to show he was more independent than Ralston had bargained for.'

'But it could have been other members of the gang who held up the stage,' Roberts pointed out. 'You've said several times that you thought there were more than the two we saw. Maybe the gang's moving out of the Territory and they need him.'

Granger was about to reply when over to his right the door from the street opened. Cora stood in the doorway, the light behind her throwing her face in shadow. She ignored Amy Morgan and Roberts, speaking directly to Granger.

'Matt, I have to talk with you,' she said.

She turned on her heel, and closed the door. In the office there was a moment's silence, Granger stood still, conscious that Amy Morgan was looking directly at him. He could see Cora waiting on the boardwalk her back to the window.

'I'll be at the house later,' he said briskly. 'You might wanna read those notes, Mr Roberts, an' think about 'em.'

He picked up his Stetson from the counter, feeling as if Amy Morgan's eyes were on his back as he crossed the office to open the door and step out into the morning light.

'What's so all fire important you had to come lookin' for me?' Granger asked as Cora turned to face him. 'I tol' you Billy comin' back was goin' to be all right.'

Cora's face was set firm. 'I want you to come with me out to the Lazy Y,' she said.

Granger looked at her, frowning. 'Is this some sort of a joke, Cora?'

Cora shook her head angrily. 'I saw Mr Ralston a couple of days ago when I was out there with Johnny Mac. Mr

Ralston's no fool, Matt, you know that. He knows that you're trouble for him, just like your pa. He wants to have a talk. Maybe work something out.'

Cora as a go-between? It was just possible. She was smart, and he recalled Macpherson telling him that Ralston thought highly of her. But Ralston was unlikely to pay much attention to any notions she had about mending fences. There was too much bad blood between Ralston and the Grangers for that.

So why should he go out to the ranch? What was in it for him? He wasn't worried about getting shot down. Ralston wasn't that crude. If the word got around that the rule of law was breaking down, folks in Cheyenne might start poking unwelcome noses into whatever Ralston was planning for Springwater.

'Mr Ralston gave me his word there'd be no trouble,' Cora said. Her hand went out and rested on Granger's arm. 'You've nothing to lose, Matt, maybe you'll gain something.'

Granger smiled. 'You always were smart, Cora. I reckon you got smarter.' He looked her up and down, taking in the long leather skirt, and the workmanlike jacket. 'Guess you changed knowin' you'd persuade me!'

Cora, smiling, pointed to the buggy drawn up in the street. 'If we leave now, we'll be back by sundown.'

They chatted together as Granger drove the Appaloosa out of the town, mainly about the changes made to the town since Granger had left. Deliberately, he avoided any topic which might lead to disagreements between them. Memories of similar buggy rides were strong. Not for the first time since returning, he wondered what might have become of them both if Charlie hadn't been killed, and Pa hadn't put him on the stagecoach to head back East where, for the first year, he had lived with a distant cousin.

Time went quickly and soon the Appaloosa was splashing through the shallow water of the river that marked the western limit of what had been Granger territory. Cora spoke for the first time for a while.

'We had some good times when you, me, an' Johnny Mac were with your ma in the schoolroom.'

She pointed towards the old Granger place, now uninhabited and beginning to take on the tell-tale signs of being abandoned. Bunch and buffalo grass had begun to reseed as it crept unimpeded over ground that had once been carefully tilled. Tall weeds thrust up from a plot close to the house where vegetables had once grown.

'You hadn't used to get whipped like me and Johnny Mac,' Granger said lightly. He deliberately turned away from the view of his old home and looked ahead once more.

'Talkin' of Johnny, how did he get the money to set up the Nugget?' he asked. 'You don't get that big a stake workin' in a sawmill.'

'I thought you knew,' Cora said. 'Johnny went South for a few years. He worked for the Indian Agency. Got into trading, made his stake, an' came back to Springwater.'

'How'd he get tied up with Ralston?'

Cora frowned. 'What do you mean?'

'That business over Billy's badge. You reckon Johnny Mac would have tried to take over without Ralston's say-so? Johnny Mac's got some link with Ralston. You sure it's Johnny Mac's money behind the Nugget?'

'That's enough, Matt!' Cora turned her head away to stare directly ahead, her lips set in a firm line. 'We need to be there in an hour if we're to be back in town before sundown.'

Granger shrugged, and flicked at the reins, prompting the Appaloosa to increase its pace.

*

The location of the big house of the Lazy Y said everything about Ralston that Granger remembered. The only two-storey building out of town, it was built on one of the few high points visible to Granger and Cora as soon as they'd reached the top of the river-bank on the western side. Not for Ralston a house in a hollow affording some protection from the harsh Wyoming winters. Instead, it rose high, commanding the lands around, as a medieval castle would have dominated its surroundings in old Europe.

The Appaloosa carried them along at a steady pace for a further hour. At one point Granger tried to start a conversation, but Cora barely answered, still irritated, it seemed, by his suggestion that Ralston's money might be behind the Nugget and not Johnny Mac's.

They'd been on Ralston's land since crossing the river, a board nailed on a stake had letters reminding them of that fact. But a mile from the big house a high archway with a board marked with burnt-black letters, hanging from chains, told visitors once more that they were on land belonging to the Lazy Y.

As the buggy approached the house, Granger could see that two large bunkhouses over to the right seemed deserted. Ralston's top-hand and his cowboys were driving Lazy Y beeves south to the railhead. Another much smaller bunkhouse stood isolated, maybe fifty yards back from a large corral, smoke coming from a metal chimney poking through the shingles. What was that remark on the stage by the reverend's wife? Was this where Ralston's men 'no better than the men they chased away' bunked down?

Following Cora's instructions, Granger drove the buggy around the corner of a large barn and then on to a path made from small stones beaten into the soil and leading to the front of the house. He could see now that the house extended maybe twenty yards long, the entrance door set in the centre flanked by two pairs of large windows. A wide covered-in porch ran the full length of the house providing relief from the summer sun.

Granger drew the buggy to a halt at the bottom of the steps which led up to the entrance door and a small man, probably a Mexican, ran down the steps to take the Appaloosa's head. Granger secured the reins, stepped down to the ground, and moved to the other side of the buggy. As he held out his hand for Cora to step down a voice from the entrance door sounded.

'You always amaze me, my dear Cora! I didn't think you'd succeed.'

Granger didn't turn, but continued to assist Cora in alighting from the buggy. He had no need to peer into the shadows around the entrance door to know that it was Ralston who'd called out. He'd remember that voice until he died, its rounded tones belonging to a man educated expensively in Europe, familiar with power and its weapons almost since he'd been out of knee-britches. For the thousandth time Granger wondered why such a man would turn to ranching in a land as harsh and as unforgiving as Wyoming.

Granger offered his arm to Cora and they ascended the steps as if they were a married couple calling on a neighbour in a city back East. Only in married couples back East, he thought wryly, the man wouldn't be armed with a Navy Colt and the woman was unlikely to be working in a saloon.

'Mr Granger,' Ralston greeted him. 'Good of you to visit.'

Neither man offered his hand. No matter what Cora had said, this meeting had been forced on Ralston by events. Granger knew Ralston was talking with him only because he judged it to be in his best interests to do so.

Ralston led them into the large entrance hall, and wordlessly pointed to the row of wooden pegs to right of the door. Two gunbelts hung side by side, their holsters weighed down with heavy sidearms. Granger unbuckled his gunbelt and hung it on the nearest peg. He had no problem with taking off his Navy. Taking a sidearm into someone's home, even Ralston's, was not something to be done.

Ralston led them through to a large room, which Granger guessed was some sort of extra parlour. The furniture, most likely imported from Europe, had the glossy surfaces only achieved after many hours of work by servants. A portrait over the wide fireplace showed the figure of a bearded man in a military uniform unfamiliar to Granger.

Ralston waved them both to chairs to the left of the fireplace in which logs burned brightly despite the mildness of the weather outside. He paused alongside a chair opposite while Cora settled her long leather skirt, and Granger took the opportunity to study the older man. Ralston had aged well, although by Granger's reckoning he was now nearing his mid-fifties. His figure was still good, his shoulders square, and his good health showed in the clearness of his eyes: ice-blue eyes, Granger recognized from all those years ago, that had never seemed to change whatever Ralston's mood.

'I'm told that young Haynes is back in office,' Ralston said. 'with your help, I understand.'

So that was the way it was to be, Granger realized. No attempt at false pleasantries, no false sympathy offered for the recent death of Pa, no offers of refreshment after a long drive. It was straight down to business.

'He'd have returned even without me,' Granger said.

Ralston looked thoughtful. 'Yes, I suppose that's true.'

As if suddenly coming to a conclusion he turned to Cora. 'My dear, I wonder if you'd be kind enough to excuse us. Midge will provide you with some refreshment. There are certain matters I need to discuss with Mr Granger.'

The two men stood up as Cora rose from her chair. 'Of course, Mr Ralston.' She turned to Granger. 'I'll wait in the buggy.'

The two men took their places after the door closed behind Cora. For a moment there was silence in the room, each man looking at each other. This is a dangerous man, and his manners and evenness of voice are mere cloaks for his greed and ruthlessness, Granger told himself. Keep that in mind, and to hell with anything else.

'You should understand, Mr Granger, that the country around here has changed from that which you may recall,' Ralston said. 'Over time I have eliminated the lawlessness that prevailed when you were a young man. Shoshone renegades and road-agents belong to the past. Springwater and the Lazy Y have been quiet and stable places these past fifteen years.' Ralston paused, as if intent on making his next words perfectly understood. 'I wish to keep it that way.'

Granger nodded. Where was Ralston heading?

'I've good friends back East,' Ralston continued. 'They tell me your employers pay you well.'

Again Granger nodded, but said nothing.

'I will pay you more, much more,' Ralston said.

'And why would you do that?'

'I've big plans for this country, Mr Granger. Your father stood in my way. I'm sure he had his reasons, but the world moves on. Join me, and I promise you'll be a rich man in five years.'

'And how would I earn it?' Granger asked. 'I don't know a cow from a coyote.'

Ralston allowed himself a brief smile. 'I've all the cowboys I need.' He looked away for a moment towards the window. 'There will be other calls on your skills.'

'You aimin' to hire my gun, Mr Ralston? I hear you got all the gunslingers a man could use.'

Ralston must have detected the hostility in Granger's voice. He turned back to stare at Granger for a few seconds. 'My men have kept the peace around this country for several years,' he said. 'That is, until you returned.'

'You sayin' I held up the stagecoach myself?'

'Maybe you were the target, Mr Granger. Road-agents might well consider it worth attacking a man whom they'd been told was carrying gold pieces.'

'I was carryin' 'em in the livery barn. The no-goods there ignored 'em. Makes me wonder why.'

Was there a flicker of something in those ice-blue eyes? Maybe time was taking its toll on Ralston, after all. 'That owlhoot I brought in from the stage,' Granger continued, 'I've been told he'd been seen rustling some of your cattle. You've got a reputation for givin' neck-tie parties for such no-goods.'

Ralston pursed his lips. 'That was a long time ago, Mr Granger, when I judged it necessary to make some examples. Nowadays, I leave such matters to Judge Parker.'

'So it wasn't your gunslingers who broke him outa jail?'

If Ralston took offence at Granger's blunt question, his eyes, or the expression on his face, gave no indication. Instead, he looked away from Granger once more towards the long window which gave him a fine view of the land surrounding the Lazy Y big house. There was a moment's silence in the room.

Ralston looked back at Granger. 'I understand that

you've made a friend of Mrs Morgan.'

Granger frowned, puzzled by Ralston's sudden change of topic. 'She's a fine woman.'

Ralston nodded. 'She is, indeed, but she seems determined to carry on what she sees as her late father's work. Caleb White, for reasons I've never understood, set himself against me.'

'Maybe he reckoned God-fearin' folks in Springwater had a right to lead their own lives without interference. As did my pa.'

'Yes, your father, also. But to be blunt, both men are dead. We're now speaking of Mrs Morgan,' Ralston said. 'I'm told that were she to lose the *Reporter* and that grand house in town, she would be left penniless.' He again looked out through the window, as he continued. 'Those men who bushwhacked you in the livery barn must still be close by. My men will find them eventually, of course, but who knows what might happen before they're caught. You might care to remind her of that.'

When Cora had asked him to visit the Lazy Y Granger had told himself that Ralston wasn't crude enough to have him shot down. But the threat against Amy was as crude as it got. He wasn't sure how Amy would react to what he was about to say, but he was going to say it, anyway.

'I can save your men work,' he said. 'Anyone harmin' Amy Morgan or the *Reporter* will have to face me. I'll hunt 'em down, an' kill 'em.'

He didn't give Ralston a chance to respond, instead getting to the only reason for his agreeing to accompany Cora to the Lazy Y.

'The old Granger homestead, I want it back. I'll give you twice what you paid the bank. The money can be here in a month.'

Ralston raised his eyebrows. 'Maybe you're paid better

than I've heard,' he said. 'But the homestead is not for sale. My purchase was legal, and I'm not even prepared to discuss it.' His mouth twitched. 'But I never suspected you of sentiment, Mr Granger.'

Granger ignored the jibe. 'Jack Daley an' my sister worked hard on that old place. You called in Jack's paper only 'cos my pa, when he was sheriff, stood against you. He wouldn't do your biddin' so after he was dead you took it out on Jack. Now Billy Haynes is provin' the same as my pa, an' that's why you tried to get rid of him a coupla nights back.'

Granger got to his feet. 'I made a mistake comin' out here. You haven't changed, Ralston. You're railroadin' the town, you're out to destroy Amy Morgan an' the paper, an' you're usin' a gang of no-goods to get whatever you're aimin' for.'

Ralston had got older, after all. As he, too, stood up, his eyes were clouded, his face white with fury. 'How dare you speak to me in that manner in my own house! I'm warning you now, Granger! Try and fill your father's boots and you'll be a dead man within a month. Good day!'

Ralston swung around and marched to the door, sending it crashing to a close behind him. Granger stood there gazing at the door as it quivered slightly on its hinges.

'Now what the hell are you hidin'?' Granger said aloud to the empty room.

CHAPTER SEVEN

'That was a good job you did with those plates, Mr Wilkins,' Granger said, counting coins into the hand of the livery-barn owner.

'Any time, Mr Granger. I got a special deal you wanna leave your palomino end o' the good weather.'

Granger smiled and shook his head. 'I ain't aimin' to be 'round here that long, Mr Wilkins.'

Wilkins made a mouth. 'That's a shame, folks were hopin'. . . .' He broke off, looking awkward. 'Anyways, if there's anythin' I can do for you, Mr Granger, you only gotta ask.'

'Thanks, I'll remember that.' Granger paused for a moment. 'There is somethin'. I s'pose you were here that morning when my pa was killed.'

'Sure I was. An' that was a bad day for Springwater. Your pa did some mighty fine things for this town.'

'Mr Macpherson was here, so I heard.'

'That's right. He came in to ask me about Miss Cora's pony.'

'You sure it was the same day?'

'Sure I'm sure, Mr Granger. I remember it well, 'cos the mayor was comin' across at noon, an' he's a real stickler for time. I asked Mr Macpherson the hour from that fancy timepiece of his when he got it out to take a look.'

'You remember the time?'

'Ten off noon.'

Granger nodded, and glanced to his left as the light changed at the edge of his vision. The boy who worked for Wilkins stood at the door.

'The buggy's ready, Mr Granger.'

'That's fine, Tommy. You still lookin' fer that no-good who gave you that message?'

'I sure am.' The boy dropped his eyes, and shuffled his feet. 'I'm really sorry, Mr Granger. . . .'

'Forget it, Tommy. Not your fault,' interrupted Granger. 'Here, catch!'

He flipped a coin to the boy who looked up quickly to shoot out a hand and catch it.

'Thanks, Mr Granger!' Tommy went scampering away to spend his good luck. Granger turned back to Wilkins.

'You're sure it was ten off noon?'

'I'm sure. An' I knowed Mr Macpherson's timepiece was right 'cos I was in the bank that mornin'. He was in there talkin' to Mr Fells an' I saw him settin' his timepiece right with the bank's clock. That clock used to be the best in town afore those no-goods shot it up.'

Granger took a coin from his pocket, and gave it to the livery owner. 'You've been a great help, Mr Wilkins. I'm obliged to you.'

Ten minutes later he drew the buggy to a halt outside the office of the *Reporter*. He was stepping down to the hardpack when Amy Morgan appeared from the newspaper offices. The light caught her face as she stepped from the shadows. He looked up at her, his pleasure showing in his expression. She had a smile that made Granger hope she was anticipating the drive as much as he was. As she reached the bottom of the steps he touched a finger to his Stetson before taking her hand to lead her around to the other side of the buggy.

'A good day for a drive, Mrs Morgan,' he said, handing her up to her seat as if she were delicate china.

'Better than your drive to the Lazy Y, Mr Granger?' Amy Morgan asked, a mischievous smile showing in the curve of her lips.

'A darn sight better, Mrs Morgan,' Granger said, his smile broadening as he walked around to step up and sit beside her. 'You mind if we take a look at the old Granger homestead afore our picnic?'

'No, of course not.'

'Polly promised me she'd made up the best basket since—'

He stopped suddenly, his smile vanishing as he remembered what Polly had said. That was a damnfool way for him to start a drive for a picnic! He turned towards Amy Morgan intending to apologize for his lack of tact but before he could speak she reached out to touch briefly Granger's hand holding the reins.

'I've not been on a picnic since the war,' she said. 'That's far too long a time. I'm looking forward to it.'

Relieved by Amy Morgan's response, Granger's smile returned. He flicked the reins and urged the pony forward.

Granger halted the buggy some fifty yards from his old home. From what he'd seen on his drive to the Lazy Y he was sure that the place was abandoned. If anyone was living there they would have challenged him by now. But with Amy, as he was beginning to think of her, alongside him, he was taking no chances.

'The place looks deserted,' Amy said.

'I think so, but I'll take a look first.' He handed the reins across to her, and stepped down. With one hand resting easily on the butt of his Navy he crossed the fifty yards to the door. He called out as he reached his old home.

'Anybody here?'

There was no response, and he pushed at the door. It swung back on squeaking hinges, and he peered inside. Save for the layers of dust, Jack and Katy might have stepped out to visit town only a few minutes before. A quick glance around convinced him that nobody had set foot in the house since they'd left.

Granger turned and waved Amy forward, waiting until she brought the buggy to a halt. As she secured the reins, and hauled on the brake to prevent the pony from wandering away, he moved forward to extend his hand. As she stepped lightly to the ground he caught the scent of fresh flowers.

'Place is covered in dust,' he said. 'Maybe you want to stay outside.'

She shook her head. 'I called here once when Billy's mother was alive.' She stepped past him to walk to the middle of the main room of the house. 'She told me your own mother had made such a good home it was easy for her to keep.'

Granger nodded. He had fond memories of his own mother, a well-educated woman who had made sure that he and Katy were schooled as best as she was able. Her teaching had stood him in good stead when he'd gone East and made efforts to study more. She'd died before her time, a year before he'd left Springwater. But Pa had been lucky to have her with him for almost twenty years. Thinking of his dead father prompted a puzzled look to show on his face.

'There's somethin' mighty peculiar about Pa's shootin',' he said.

'What do you mean?'

'I was talkin' with Fells at the bank. He tol' me that those no-goods had got the money they came for. Then, just as they were leavin', one of 'em turned at the door and put a shot through the clock.'

'To frighten anyone from following, I imagine,' Amy said.

'Yeah, maybe. But up to that moment they were getting away with the robbery. Maybe they knew that Jenkins, the sheriff before Billy, was outa town. So why stir up the townsfolk an' maybe have some young feller charge out an' try an' stop them?'

Granger stopped suddenly. 'Unless . . .' he said slowly. Then he shook his head as if dismissing a thought. 'Anyways, their plans sure went ornery when Johnny Mac appeared.' His mouth twisted. 'I don't trust Johnny Mac an inch but he'd be a good man in a shoot-out.'

He looked thoughtfully at Amy. 'You know what goes on in Springwater. How much was Pa involved in the town after he finished being sheriff?'

'As much as he ever had been,' she replied. 'The councilmen often asked his advice. Jenkins was always asking for his help.'

Granger frowned. 'I'm gonna think some more about this.' Deliberately changing the subject he swung around waving an outstretched ann. 'It's mighty strange to me now that a whole family could live in this space. Yet I had happy times here. Pa and me, we used to fight old Indian Wars around and under the table. Ma would always end up hollerin' at both of us!'

Amy laughed aloud. 'You mean your father went under the table as well?'

'Sure, he did. He used to wriggle on his belly under the table and crawl to the chimney. He'd leave messages in a loose brick an' I had to fight my way through Sioux on the warpath an' collect them.'

Granger swung around to the fireplace. 'Hey! I just wonder!'

A couple of strides took him across the room, his steps outlined in the dust that covered the boards. He squatted down before the cold fireplace, ashes and sticks on the hearth still showing signs of the last fire.

Reaching forward, he pulled at a stone. Nothing moved. His memory must be playing tricks. But maybe he was on the wrong line. He reached higher up the chimney and tugged. The heavy square stone came away in his hand. Behind it rested a leather pouch.

He stood up, holding the pouch in the air. 'Messages for the fort!'

Granger was jokingly triumphant. 'After all these years! Pa must have forgotten all about this, an' I reckon Katy was too young to remember.'

Amy laughed aloud, and Granger wondered if she knew just how fine she looked with her head tilted back, the line of her chin and throat taut, her fair hair swept up beneath a small hat.

'What in tarnation we got here?' Granger said looking down at the opened pouch. He took out a sheet of paper, staring down at it, a frown appearing on his face as he read what the paper said.

'A message for the cavalry?' Amy asked mischievously.

Granger looked up from the paper, his expression serious. 'It's a letter to Pa, dated only a coupla months ago.'

He crossed the room to the table, using his hand to brush away the dust, and laid the paper down. 'Come an' look at this.'

Together, heads close, they read the letter. It bore the salutation '*To my loyal comrade at arms, Albert Granger.* The wording of the letter, brief to the point of bluntness, stated that '*the matter will be investigated*'.

'What could that refer to, I wonder? And I don't understand the meaning of the signature,' Amy said.

'Me neither,' said Granger. He read the signature aloud. '*Donehogawa of the Iroquois.*'

What the hell was all this about? The letter looked genuine, although for some reason there was no hint as to where the letter had originated. His father had been in blue uniform during the war, but he'd been with the engineers. He wouldn't even have seen an Iroquois, and he sure wouldn't be getting letters from one, especially written in such a fine copperplate hand.

The only Indians his father had ever dealt with, as far as Granger knew, were the Shoshone when they lived on the lands now occupied by the Lazy Y. But that was years ago, when he and Macpherson were still in britches and stockings.

'Could your father have written this for some reason? Still playing a game of some sort?'

'This isn't the hand of any o' my folks, an' Jack Daley ain't that well-lettered.'

'Billy's mother, perhaps?'

Granger managed a wry smile. 'Pa wrote me an' said Billy's ma was a lovin' woman, but she hadn't read a word since her MacGuffey's *Reader* in the schoolroom.'

He picked up the letter and folded it carefully, placing it in an inside secret pocket of his trail jacket, now empty. His gold coins had been locked away in the safe at Amy's house.

'I think it's time we had our picnic,' Granger said. He'd think more about the letter at a later time.

'There's a beautiful spot a mile or two along the riverbank. We could go there,' Amy said. A small frown appeared on her face. 'Do you think this letter is connected with your father's death?'

'I don't see how it can be,' Granger admitted. 'But I'm gonna try an' find out!'

Granger settled the basket at the rear of the buggy, and walked round to step up to his seat and unhitch the reins. He felt as if he'd not need to eat for a couple of days.

'That was the biggest picnic I've ever seen,' Granger said. 'Polly musta given us enough food for twenty! You've got some fine people workin' in your house.'

Amy nodded agreement as the buggy began to move away from the shade of the trees at the edge of the river bank. The pony stepped out into a trot and Granger reckoned that after a mile or so they'd pick up a regular track into Springwater. He was hoping Billy would be around. Maybe he could shed some light on what had been found behind the chimney stone, but if Billy had known about the letter surely he'd have mentioned it.

They sat close to each other, both content to enjoy the warm afternoon, and the aftermath of a good meal. Polly had put in a couple of flasks of French wine, taken, she'd told Granger, from the last of the wine kept by Caleb White, Amy's father. Polly had looked at Granger directly when she'd handed him the basket.

'You don't mind my sayin', Mr Matt,' she'd said, 'plenty o' fellers have asked Miss Amy to go on a picnic, but she ain't never gone before.'

'Perhaps Billy might know something about the letter?' Amy said, breaking the silence.

'That's what I've been thinkin',' he said.

He hauled back suddenly on the reins bringing the buggy to a halt. He took the reins in one hand, his right hand shifting to rest on the butt of his Navy, his eyes looking across the ground ahead of the buggy.

'What's wrong?' Amy asked.

'You see those cottonwoods? Shift fifty yards down the slope. Two men on the ground.'

Amy looked towards where Granger was pointing. 'Yes! I see them!' She paused. 'Are they sleeping?'

The long sleep, Granger thought, but didn't say it. 'I think we'd better take a look.' He turned to Amy. 'You OK with that?'

She nodded, her lips pressed together. He urged the pony forward, the buggy rattling off the soil of the track, the wheels cutting through the bunch and buffalo grass. A hundred yards or so from the track Granger slowed the buggy to a walk, finally halting some twenty yards away from where the men were on the ground. He was close enough to see blood on the jacket of one of the men.

'You should turn your head away,' he said.

'I've seen dead men before,' she said quietly. 'I'm not afraid.'

Granger secured the reins, and stepped down. His eyes ranged around as he approached where the men lay. Both men were plainly dressed, black suits, and beneath their coats, black vests over rough grey shirts. A small black leather-covered book was clutched in one of the men's hands. Their identical hats lay a few feet away, one showing its brim soaked with blood.

Granger looked around, but no loose horses were to be seen. The men looked as if they'd been bushwhacked but their modest clothing gave no suggestion that they were worth robbing. Granger breathed in deeply. There was nothing he could do here. The ground was within Billy's territory and he'd tell his stepbrother what he'd found when he got to town. Somebody would come out and pick up the bodies. The thought struck him that Ralston's rule of law in the territory was breaking down. He had turned to go back to the buggy, when the voice rang out.

'Hold it right there, Granger!'

Granger moved fast, bringing his Navy up to extend it at arm's length, aiming at the point in the cottonwoods from where the voice had come. Again the voice rang out.

'You put that cannon down, right now, Granger!'

The caller was hidden between the closely set trunks of the cottonwoods, and Granger turned sideways, making himself a smaller target.

'I got two men up here with long guns. They're aimin' at that woman o' yourn. You got five seconds to put that sidearm down!'

Granger paused. Was the caller bluffing? Maybe the man was alone.

'Two seconds, Granger!'

He wasn't going to take the chance. He lowered his Navy, and stood still.

'Don't make a run for it, lady!' The unseen man shouted. 'Or my men will shoot! Put your sidearm on the ground, Granger, an' step away.'

He had no option. The caller might be bluffing but he couldn't take the chance with Amy's life. These were the killers of the men on the ground, he guessed. They'd not care who they killed if it meant they could save themselves.

There was movement at the edge of the cottonwoods, and a man carrying a long gun, stepped forward away from the trees. Granger saw him wave a hand, and branches of trees over to Granger's right bent over as two men jumped to the ground. Both carried long guns.

As the three moved down the slope towards Granger, he recognized one of them as the outlaw he'd brought into Springwater after the attempted stage robbery. The other two he hadn't seen before.

The one who'd called from the trees, a battered derby

hat on his head, fair hair falling to his shoulders, appeared to be the leader, the other two allowing him to walk maybe a couple of paces ahead of them. He reached Granger's Colt, not shifting his eyes, and bent to pick up the sidearm. He made a great show of examining it before looking up again at Granger.

'Now ain't this a surprise! The dude from back East! Never thought to meet up with you this fine afternoon.'

'Let the woman go,' Granger said. 'You've no fight with her.'

The leader of the three bared his teeth in a humourless smile, and turned to the man alongside him. 'Ike, you go and grab the buggy pony an' bring that fine lady over here.'

'Sure, Nathan!'

Ike, Granger realized, must be the speaker's brother. He had the same angular features, and similar brown eyes, although Ike's face was marked by a scar that ran from his eyebrow to the corner of his mouth. Ike walked briskly towards where Amy sat motionless in the buggy. Leading the animal's head, he brought it back to stand alongside the man called Nathan.

'Take a look at the dude's arm,' said Ike suddenly, as if remembering something he'd been told. 'Don't he carry a knife?'

Immediately Nathan stepped forward, his acid-smelling breath reaching Granger's nostrils. His hand closed around Granger's forearms in turn.

'He ain't got no knife today,' he said.

'I'm askin' agin,' Granger said. 'Let the lady go. She's got nothin' to do with any o' this.'

Nathan leered in Amy's direction. 'Now I wouldn't jest put it like that, Granger, 'cos I hear a different story.' He scratched his unshaven chin with the barrel of Granger's

Navy, making a great show of turning over his thoughts before he spoke.

'Question I gotta answer is what do I do with you now?'

'What we waitin' for? This dude knifed Frank!' The stagecoach attacker spat out. 'Kill 'im now!' His face split in a leer. 'We'll keep the woman alive.'

'Slow down, Jesse!' Nathan snapped. 'I got some thinkin' to do.'

Nathan took a step back, bringing up his long gun. 'Get in that buggy, Granger. You an' the woman gonna be our guests tonight!'

CHAPTER EIGHT

Granger had been driving the buggy for almost two hours, following Ike as he'd been ordered, when they crossed a track and headed towards thick woods of pine. Ike turned in his saddle and looked beyond the buggy to where Nathan, the leader in the battered derby hat, was riding alongside the stagecoach bandit called Jesse.

'Hold it, Ike,' Nathan shouted. He urged his mount forward, closing the buggy to draw alongside Granger.

'Ike's gonna lead you through the pines,' he said. 'You maybe don't think you'll make it with the buggy, but we done it before.' He looked past Granger to leer at Amy who stared straight ahead. 'We're gonna spend the night together. Ain't that nice?'

He laughed coarsely, and turned away. 'OK, Ike, take it good and slow,' he called out.

Ike turned his mount's head, keeping the horse at a walk, bending low in his saddle as he rode forward to break through the low hanging branches of the pines.

'Get your head low,' Granger said to Amy. 'Try an' keep your shoulder forward.'

He turned the buggy pony to follow Ike through the gap between the trunks, on the outer edge of the dense stand of trees. They fended off low-hanging branches brushing against them as the buggy found just room enough to penetrate the closely packed trees. Fifty yards from the outer ring of pines, in the shadowy interior of the wood, Granger could see that trees had been felled ahead of them making it easier for the buggy to follow the track.

For maybe ten minutes they rode along in silence, Granger desperately trying to think of a way of enabling Amy to escape. Ike, he thought, might be the weak spot of the gang, eager to follow Nathan's orders. But with Nathan and the outlaw called Jesse watching him all the time he knew his chances weren't good. Fury welled up within himself as he was forced to recognize his helplessness. He cursed himself for bringing this danger to Amy. Save for the few words she'd spoken when he got back in the buggy she'd remained silent. He knew she must be desperately afraid of what these men intended.

Would they kill her after they'd finished with her? Maybe not. He remembered Nathan's words when he'd ordered them to follow Ike. He'd said something about having thinking to do. Nathan hadn't expected to come across him and Amy today, of that he was certain. Maybe the three men had been out looking to rob anyone they met. That would explain the two dead men. But what about Ralston's claim that he'd sent all the no-goods packing? First the bank, then the raid on the stage, his own beating, now this. Was Ralston, for his own reasons, allowing these men to kill and loot as the chance arose? Or were they on Ralston's payroll following his orders?

The buggy burst through a swathe of low lying branches and into a clearing, now in shadow as the daylight began to fade, and the darkness of night crept in. Over to his left a small corral held a couple of horses staring impassively at them across the open ground. On the far side of the clearing stood a rough dwelling, built with wattle and daub, stout timbers strengthening the corners. Dried mud and clods of bunch and buffalo grass covered the roofing from which a metal pipe protruded; thin grey smoke being carried away by the light wind which rustled the pine leaves. Granger grimaced. Were there yet more men inside? If that was the case, their chances of survival were even less than he'd reckoned. He let go the reins to cover Amy's hand with his own. She turned to look at him, her lips trembling, the fear showing in her eyes.

Their three captors dismounted, and Nathan moved to stand by the buggy, his hand resting on the butt of his sidearm.

'Get down, an' no trouble.'

His left hand went out to assist Amy, but she turned her head away from Nathan's gaze and stepped down unaided. Jesse on the other side of the buggy, his sidearm held down by his leg, moved back a pace as Granger secured the reins and stepped down.

'Now, ain't this friendly,' Nathan said in a mock cheerful voice. 'Shame we gotta tie you up, Granger. This here lady's gonna be cookin' our supper, an' I know you're just bound to cause trouble.'

Amy whirled on the speaker. 'I wouldn't boil a pan of water for you! You foul beast!'

Nathan threw his head back, and laughed loudly. 'That I am!' he roared.

But then his expression changed, and he grabbed Amy roughly by her arm, his grimy fingers digging into the soft flesh below her coat.

'You're gonna do what I want, you un'erstand? An' I'm gonna want plenty!'

Amy tore her arm from his grasp and, sucking in her cheeks, spat directly into his face. Nathan stood still, spittle dripping from his cheekbone, his face as black as the sky of a prairie storm. He savagely scrubbed away the spittle with the back of his hand, and then the same hand flashed out, striking Amy hard against the side of her face, knocking her to the ground.

Granger stepped forward only to halt as the barrel of Jesse's sidearm was rammed hard against the nape of his neck. For a second there was silence in the clearing; Amy, on the ground, her face hidden, Nathan, his hand raised as if to strike her again, glaring down at her.

'Nathan, there's no need for this,' Granger said quickly. 'There's food in the basket back o' the buggy. Good food, and enough for all of you.'

Nathan lowered his arm, and turned to face Granger. 'Lemme see that.'

He moved to the rear of the buggy, and lifted the basket to set it on the ground. With scrabbling fingers he undid the leather straps, and threw back the lid, letting out a shout of glee.

'Fer Chris'sakes, look at this good grub!' He held up a bottle. 'What the hell's this stuff? Is it liquor?'

'Fine French wine,' Granger said. Thank God, Polly hadn't put in whiskey. 'Same as they drink back East.'

Nathan looked at the bottle again, before raising it to his mouth. His blackened teeth closed over the cork and he spat it on to the ground. Then he lifted the bottle and took a cautious sip.

'It ain't nothin' like whiskey but it ain't bad,' he announced.

Granger breathed in deeply, silently blessing Polly's over-generous provisioning for the picnic. Maybe the basket had bought him a few hours to think of something.

Nathan, the bottle clutched in his hand, moved back to stand alongside Amy who was slowly getting to her feet. A deep red patch showed on the side of her face where Nathan had struck her. He took hold of her wrist, and this

84

time she didn't struggle, although she pulled her face away as he leaned towards her.

'You got three minutes behind the cabin to do whatever you gotta do. You take any longer an' I'm gonna come lookin' fer you.'

He pushed her away, and swung around to Granger who stood motionless, Jesse's pistol still against his neck.

'You, Granger, go into them trees where we can see you. I ain't having you foulin' the cabin tonight.'

Granger felt the sidearm removed from his neck. What was Nathan's game? Why was he putting them both in the cabin? Unless it was some vicious plan of Nathan's there should be several hours for him to think how he and Amy might escape. Granger turned and walked into the trees, thankful to be alive.

The stink from the rough blankets on the bunk stung his nostrils and he threw them aside to lie on the straw-filled mattress, aware from the sounds that Amy, across the other side of the room, was doing something similar. The straw rustled as she settled on to the mattress.

He lay there staring up at the dark. Since being bundled into the cabin, and the door being secured behind them, he'd tried to comfort Amy. But how could mere words comfort this woman he admired so much? He knew that despite her silence she must be terrified of what tomorrow would bring.

How did he, himself, feel about the coming of daylight? He knew their only hope lay in the fact that Nathan and his men hadn't killed them immediately. Would Nathan try and extort money in exchange for their lives? He remembered when he was a boy a bunch of renegade Shoshone taking a couple of white women and wanting gold in exchange. His father and a couple of deputies had killed every one of them and released the women.

The silence of the room was broken by the sound of muffled weeping from across the room. Godamnit to hell! If he'd never come back to Springwater, Amy would never have ended up in this stinking cabin.

'Can you forgive me for getting you into this?' Granger said softly.

The muffled weeping stopped. There was a pause, and then she whispered just loud enough for him to hear.

'Maybe something like this would have happened anyway, Matthew. There's nothing to forgive.'

For a brief moment a smile touched his lips.

'I'm gonna tell you about a woman I met when I was with the cavalry,' he said, deliberately keeping his voice as soft as he could. 'Ellen Johnson was her name. She was in Fort Snelling, a fine woman, with a kind and gentle husband, and a lively little son who favoured her. One of the other officers told me her history. She'd been travelling West when the wagons were hit by a Sioux war party. The men were killed an' the women taken.'

Granger paused, breathing in. 'The leader of the war party took her as his wife. His bucks took the other women. Three of the women killed themselves, some got sick and died, a couple lost their minds. Ellen Johnson learned from the squaws, did her work as best she could, and made friends. When she was called to his tepee she went without complaint, and washed herself in the river next morning. A year later a cavalry troop caught up with the Sioux. When the fightin' was over Ellen Johnson walked out to meet them, her head held high. An officer asked her how she'd survived. She smiled, and said "I chose to live".'

There was silence in the cabin for several seconds, and Granger stared into the darkness above him wondering if maybe it would have been better to have kept his mouth shut.

'I'm not sure I'm that strong,' Amy whispered finally.

'Yes, you are,' he said. 'You've been showing that since your husband was killed and your father died. Maybe I'll not make it tomorrow, but you can.' He stared hard at the darkness above him. She'd called him by his name, and he knew he'd think about that to the very end.

'Amy, you'll have to live both our lives for us.'

He heard a sob, and cursed himself for his bluntness, but he knew he'd said the right things. 'Remember Ellen Johnson,' he said. A few minutes later he heard her steady breathing, and guessed she was asleep.

CHAPTER NINE

'You bin holdin' out o' me, fancy lady! You might wanna give Ike here a few lessons in cookin' later on!' Nathan shovelled in the last of his beans, chewing them with an open mouth before taking a long noisy slurp of coffee from his tin cup.

'Ain't that right, dude?' Nathan called. 'Fancy lady's gonna make us happy, ain't she?'

Nathan looked across to where Granger was seated on the ground, his back against a pine. His legs were stretched out before him, his arms behind him around the trunk of the tree, his hands firmly tied.

'Hey, dude! I'm talkin' to you! Cat got your tongue 'cos you ain't had no coffee?'

'I hear you, Nathan,' Granger said.

He saw that Nathan had almost finished his breakfast. Silently, Amy had served the three men as they lounged around the embers of the fire they'd lit to warm themselves the previous night. Around them were strewn the remains of the picnic food from the basket. A chunk of fruit cake had been mashed by someone's boot. The wine bottle lay empty against a stone.

Nathan got to his feet, looking in his direction, and Granger felt his muscles tense. Whatever Nathan had planned was going to happen in the next few minutes.

Again he tried to force his hands apart, ignoring the searing pain where the rough rope had torn through his skin. But it was no use. The outlaw Jesse knew his business, and there was no chance of breaking free.

Nathan was giving orders to Ike. 'Now you got that straight, little brother? Me an' Jesse are gonna be back by sundown. If missy here tries to run, you make sure you catch her. Then you can whup 'er.' He stared hard at the young man. 'But you keep your hands off her, you un'erstand what I mean?'

Ike swallowed. 'Sure, Nathan.'

Nathan grabbed the younger man by his arm and thrust his face forward. 'An' stay right away from that dude. You don't untie him for nothin'. Nothin' at all! You got that?'

'What happens he wants to go in the woods?'

'He does it in his pants.' Nathan swung away. 'C'mon Jesse, soon's we get done the better.'

'Nathan!' Ike suddenly sounded anxious. 'What happens you an' Jesse don't come back.'

Beside his horse, Nathan turned back to his brother. 'Don't you fuss, little brother! Me an' Jesse'll be back.' He paused and looked first at Amy and then around at Granger before looking at his brother once more.

'But if we ain't, you kill 'em both!'

Granger watched the two men mount, and urge their horses towards the gap in the pines which would lead them out of the wood. Where were they going and what had Nathan to do? Would they return at sundown with orders to kill them both? Or had Nathan remembered the stage was due in Springwater today? Maybe he and Jesse were aiming for the mailbag once more.

He looked across to Amy who was picking up the pans, and placing them ready for scouring. The red stain on the side of her face was beginning to turn blue. Ike sat on a fallen log, his hand loosely resting on his sidearm. He looked vaguely fearful, as if, with his brother and Jesse gone, he was thinking that somehow Granger would untie himself and fall on him to wreak vengeance.

Maybe half an hour passed, Granger's eyes following Amy as she moved around the camp. She had barely glanced at him that morning, save for taking his hand briefly as they had emerged from the cabin at sun-up. Nathan had allowed her to go behind the cabin while he and Jesse were lashing his hands around the back of the pine. He found it hard to guess what she was thinking. Her expression gave nothing away.

He watched her emerge from the cabin door and look towards Ike who remained sitting on the log. 'Ike! I'm making more coffee. Would you care for some?'

'I sure would, ma'am.' Ike's expression changed as if he'd reminded himself that he shouldn't be so polite to his prisoner. 'Yeah, make more coffee,' he said gruffly.

'I'll bring it to you, Ike,' she said.

There was something about the way she said Ike's name that made Granger look hard at her back as she re-entered the cabin. Was she planning something? Surely she wasn't going to try and attack Ike? Should she try that, Ike would have all the excuse he needed to do what he liked with her, regardless of the warning from his brother.

A few minutes later Amy reappeared carrying two steaming tin cups of coffee. She walked across to the log and handed Ike a cup. Then to Granger's surprise she sat down on the log alongside him. Ike, from his expression, equally surprised, moved a few inches to give her skirts more room.

Granger continued to watch as the two sat sipping their coffee, as if they were companions seated at a table in the Springwater hotel. At one point Ike opened his mouth to speak, then appeared to change his mind, and it was Amy who broke the silence.

'Couldn't you give Mr Granger some coffee? He'll not get breakfast but it's hard to go without coffee.'

Ike reacted as if stung. He leapt to his feet, almost upending the tin cup, coffee spilling to the ground. 'No! He ain't gettin' nothin' from me. You heard what Nathan said!'

'Ike, please! Your brother will never know. Mr Granger can't cause you trouble.'

Ike's face was red with anger. 'I done tol' you! I ain't goin' near him!'

Amy let out a long sigh. 'I understand. After all, Mr Granger is a dangerous man. Even your brother said that.'

Stung by her implied accusation, Ike threw his tin mug to the ground.

'Now you listen to me! I ain't scared o' Granger! I'm doin' what Nathan said an' keepin' away.'

Amy nodded. 'I'm sorry, Ike. I forgot what your brother said.' She smiled up at him, deliberately allowing her gaze, it appeared to Granger, to linger on Ike's face.

'Could I give him coffee? You know I'll not be trouble or you'll come after me.'

Granger licked his lips. Coffee wouldn't set him free, but it would sure help him get through the day, although he hated to see Amy humiliate herself before this trail-trash just so he could get a few gulps of coffee. He hoped to hell she wasn't overplaying her hand. If Ike once got the idea she was there for the taking, his brother's warning wouldn't be worth spit on a rock.

'You just remember what I'll do to you, you give me trouble!' Ike shouted. 'All right, give him coffee.'

Amy stood up, her face calm. 'Thank you,' she said.

She turned towards Granger and walked across the

clearing towards him. Granger saw that Ike was watching her the whole way. She reached Granger and dropped to her knees, her skirts falling against his outstretched legs. Her face was only a few inches from his, her upper body touching the surface of his shirt.

'Coffee, Mr Granger,' she said loudly.

With one hand she raised the cup to his lips. Gratefully, he sipped at the black liquid, now only tepid. A sudden sting in his hand caused him to twitch violently, almost dislodging the cup from his lips.

'Oh God! Have I cut you?' Amy whispered, and he realized that her free arm was around the back of the pine. She'd got a knife from somewhere!

'Cut away,' he mumbled, his lips away from the cup.

'You're takin' too long!' Ike shouted from across the clearing.

'Coming, Ike,' Amy called back.

With a sudden jerk, Granger felt the ropes holding his hands part, and Amy brought her hand, now free of the knife, from around the tree and placed it beneath the cup.

'Go in the cabin, an' make as if—' Granger said.

'I know what you mean,' she said quickly. Against the blue of the bruise, her face coloured pink. Avoiding his eyes, she got to her feet and turned away. Slowly she walked across the clearing holding the cup in both hands.

Granger remained still, careful not to move his shoulders. If Ike walked across to check on the ropes he'd have to make a grab for the knife behind the tree. Amy reached the ashes of the fire, bending to pick up the tin cup that Ike had thrown down in his anger. He'd taken his seat on the log again but she didn't look in his direction, walking past him to pick up the three pans the men had used at breakfast.

Finally, she reached the cabin, turning briefly to look in

his direction before disappearing from Granger's view. He'd give her a few minutes, and then make his move. If Ike suddenly started for the cabin he'd rush him across the clearing, taking his chances against Ike's sidearm.

'Thanks for the coffee, Ike,' he called.

'Weren't nothin' to do with me,' Ike replied. 'Thank that woman o' yourn.'

For a crazy moment Granger was tempted to call out that yes, indeed, she is my woman. Instead he called out, 'You got it wrong, Ike. She ain't nothin' to me.'

'She brung you coffee.'

'Sure she did. Maybe she didn't want me tellin' you 'bout Nathan an' her in that cabin.'

Ike stood up from the log. 'What you talkin' 'bout?'

'Your brother holdin' out on you, Ike?'

'Nathan tells me everythin'! You like talkin' in riddles?'

'You musta been sleepin' when Nathan came into the cabin. Stayed awhile an' that fancy lady never made a sound. Thought he might have tol' you.'

'You're godamned lyin'!'

'OK, have it your way, Ike.'

Ike took a step forward in his direction, and Granger scrabbled behind the tree, trying to find the hilt of the knife. His fingers found the blade and it stung his palm. The knife was sharp, but would it throw straight? He'd have one chance only, and if he missed, Ike would almost certainly shoot him down. And then what would happen to Amy?

'You're tryin' to make trouble, Granger. You think I'm stupid?'

'I'm tryin' to do a deal, Ike, that's all.'

Ike frowned. 'You ain't in no position to make a deal.'

'You're gonna go in that cabin after her, I know it. An' Nathan wants her for hisself. I keep my mouth shut—'

'I ain't lettin' you go!' Ike shouted.

Granger shook his head. 'I ain't askin' fer that. I know Nathan'd kill you. Just say a few words when Nathan gets back.' Granger tried to smile encouragingly. 'You know, tell him that there ain't anythin' to gain by another killin'. Somethin' like that.'

He saw Ike's eyes flicker towards the cabin. Would he swallow the so-called deal? If Ike stopped to think it through he'd realize that it was full of holes but it was the best Granger could think of on the spur of the moment.

A slow lascivious grin grew on Ike's face. 'You sayin' she didn't make a sound when Nathan came for her?'

'Not a word.'

Ike turned on his heel, and walked towards the cabin door, his fingers already at his belt. Granger didn't move, and as he'd expected, Ike turned back to look at him as he reached the door. Granger saw him push through the door and disappear from view.

Granger scrambled to his feet, clenching and unclenching his fists, bending and stretching his arms so as to ease the stiffness in his limbs. He grabbed the knife from behind the pine, seeing that it was an old skinning knife with a weighted handle. As he stepped lightly across the clearing towards the cabin he balanced the knife on his palm, checking if it could be thrown with any chance of striking the target. If he caught Ike unawares, even if he missed with his throw, he might have a chance to rush him.

Silently he reached the door, seeing it was ajar enough for him to slip through. What would he see the other side? God forgive him if he'd overplayed his hand. He stepped into the shadowy interior, lit only by the morning sun creeping into the room.

For an instant he saw Amy standing by the bunk on

which he'd slept uneasily the night before. Her fingers were at the neck of her shirt, and he saw the whiteness of her shoulder and the curve of her breast. A foot away from her stood Ike, his open trail pants on his hips. Maybe he saw Granger's shadow thrown across the floor of the shack, for he swung around with a cry of rage, reaching for his gunbelt he'd left on the rough table.

His hand was still inches away from the butt of his gun when the old skinning knife struck him in the chest, the blade cutting through cloth and flesh to pierce the soft tissue of his heart. For a moment Ike was motionless, as if hung on strings like a marionette. Shock was registered in his staring eyes. He took a step forward, his hands fluttering towards the hilt of the knife, before crashing face down on the floor.

Save for the mark where Nathan had struck her, Amy's face was chalk-white, her eyes screwed tight as she pulled her shirt together. She mouthed in a harsh whisper over and over again.

'O, my God! O, my God! O, My God!'

Granger went forward quickly, and threw his arms around her shoulders, holding her tight. Her head pressed hard against his chest, and she began to sob.

'It's over, Amy, it's over,' he said. 'We gotta move outa here fast!'

CHAPTER TEN

Granger was leaning against the counter in the offices of the *Reporter* watching Morley Roberts scribbling furiously with a pencil into yet another of his leather-backed notebooks. Two other books, already full, were stacked on his desk.

'Don't you go puttin' this in the paper, Morley!' Granger said. 'I'm tellin' you what happened 'cos I might need that brain o' yours to help me figure out what's goin' on 'round here.'

The young man looked up and grinned. 'You flatter me, Mr Granger. But I need these notes for my book.'

Granger reacted sharply. 'An' don't you go puttin' me in any book!'

Roberts laughed, and maybe deliberately avoided answering. He looked down at his notes again. 'And what happened finally?' he asked.

'We took off outa there, leavin' the buggy. We grabbed a coupla horses from their corral, and brought back the buggy pony with us.'

Roberts finished writing and put down his pencil. He blew air from pursed lips in a gesture of relief. 'You certainly live dangerously, Mr Granger. Thank the Lord you saved Miss Amy. How is she, by the way? I haven't seen her this morning.'

'She's shook up. But she's resting, an' in good spirits.'

The door opened behind Granger, and he turned to see his stepbrother on the threshold. Granger saw he wore on his hip a new Navy Colt. But, he decided, Billy had the look of a worried man.

'Mornin', Mr Roberts,' Billy said. 'Matt, I need your help.'

'What's wrong, Billy?'

Haynes glanced at Morley Roberts. 'This ain't for the paper yet.'

Granger frowned. 'You got ants in your pants, Billy? What's goin' on?'

Billy took a deep breath. 'Henry Fells strung hisself up in that old barn back o' the bank,' he said in a rush. 'Or maybe he ain't,' he added grimly. 'Maybe some critter gave him a helpin' hand!'

Granger picked up his trail coat from a hook. 'OK Billy, lead the way.' He turned to Morley Roberts. 'Not a word about this.'

Roberts nodded, and bent over his book again, pencil in hand.

Billy swallowed a couple of times. 'First time I seen a man strung up.'

Granger made sure that the bar to secure the door was in place before he stepped further into the barn. Dust particles danced in the sunlight streaming through the windows placed high in the barn. One beam shone directly on the slowly moving body of Henry Fells as it dangled from a rope thrown over one of the rafters. Below and a little to the left of his feet, clad in black button shoes, an overturned barrel lay on the straw-covered ground.

Granger advanced to the hanged man. From the

97

bulging eyes, and the protruding tongue, he guessed that Fells had strangled slowly, instead of the clean broken neck delivered by a professional hangman. Fells would have struggled for a minute or so, maybe trying to support himself on the rope before his arms lost their strength and the harsh noose closed hard against the flesh of his throat.

Granger pointed to the side of the barn. 'Untie the rope, Billy, I'll take this poor critter's weight.'

He stood below Fells's body, watching Billy struggle to untie the knot, and then, when the knot was finally loosened and Billy was leaning back with both hands on the rope, he called out, 'OK, I'll take him.'

As the body was lowered, Granger took the weight in his outstretched arms, easing the body on to the ground until what remained of Fells was stretched out face upwards.

'Jesus! What a terrible way to go,' Billy said, looking down at the banker's distorted face. 'I hope to hell I never see anythin' like this agin.'

'You think maybe some critter gave him a helping hand?' Granger said, kneeling down alongside the body. 'What makes you think that?'

'His hands,' Billy said. 'I saw 'em afore I came to fetch you. They're all bruised. He maybe put up a fight.'

'Your thinkin's good, Billy,' Granger said, turning over one of Fells's hands. 'But he coulda done that himself. Most times folks who do this change their minds and try to save themselves.'

He bent further towards the hand. 'But you see that mark around his wrist? You reckon it's somethin' like I got?'

Granger held up his own wrist showing Billy the seared flesh caused by the rope burns. Billy shifted to look at Fells's wrist.

'It ain't as bad as yours,' he said slowly. 'Mebbe he

didn't fight so hard against it.'

Granger stood up slowly. 'Truth is Billy, I ain't sure one way or another. I do know Fells was as jumpy as a grasshopper. He seemed really bad about sellin' Jack's paper. Mebbe he'd done other things for Ralston he felt bad about.'

Billy nodded. 'Might explain his drinkin'. He useta be such a God-fearin' man.' He looked down at the body. 'I'll get Moses Jackson across here, put Mr Fells in a casket, tell Moses to keep his mouth shut. We don't want Mrs Fells to see her husband like this.'

Granger and Billy left the barn, Billy ensuring that the door was firmly bolted, telling Granger that he'd put a sign on it telling folks to keep away. The two men had reached the end of the alleyway running alongside the bank when they turned to see Macpherson driving a wagon down Main Street. The bed of the wagon was covered in a sheet of canvas. Granger saw Macpherson haul back on the reins of a big apron-faced grey to bring the wagon to a halt outside the sheriff's office.

As Granger and Billy approached the wagon, Macpherson jumped to the ground and went up the steps to the boardwalk. He pushed against the door, and finding it locked turned around to look along Main Street.

'Over here, Johnny Mac!' Granger called.

He and Billy made the last few yards and they stepped up to the boardwalk together. 'You lookin' fer me, Mr Macpherson?' Billy asked.

Macpherson smiled broadly. 'Gotta nice surprise, for you, Billy. I just been doin' your work for you.'

'You goin' to tell me what that work is?'

Macpherson's smile slipped a little. Billy's voice indicated that he hadn't forgotten Macpherson's attempt to take over his badge. Billy was making it clear he was in no mood for pleasantries.

Macpherson pointed to the wagon. 'Take a look down there. Coupla no-goods tried to jump me an' Cora out for a buggy ride. They shoulda tried another line of business.'

Billy glanced at Granger. 'Turnin' out to be quite a day,' he said, and went down the steps.

Granger and Macpherson followed. Billy went around to the rear of the wagon, looking up both ways along the boardwalk to check that no townsfolk were near. He leaned across and jerked back the canvas, looking down for a moment before letting out a low whistle.

'One of these is that no-good Jesse Drummond I had in the cage.'

Granger pushed past Macpherson to take a better look at the two bodies. Alongside the body of Drummond lay the outlaw known to Granger only as Nathan. Partly obscuring the bloodstained front of his shirt the battered derby hat sat on his chest. Macpherson's idea of a joke, he supposed.

Had the two men returned to their hideout and found the body of Ike? Surely they couldn't have mistaken Macpherson and Cora for himself and Amy making their escape? The questions kept piling up. Why had Nathan ridden away that morning at the hideout? He suspected they were going for orders, and that surely meant Ralston had a hand in this somewhere. But where exactly and why, was beginning to make Granger think he was staggering around in the dark.

'I've seen the other one before,' he said. 'This Drummond trash called him Nathan. I never heard his other name. These no-goods attacked me and Mrs Morgan a couple of days ago.'

'Well, they sure ain't gonna attack anybody ever again.' Billy looked at Macpherson. 'I'm obliged to you,' he said briskly. 'I'll have 'em shifted, an' get the wagon back to you.'

A half-smile on his face, Macpherson nodded. 'Glad to be of service, Sheriff.' He turned to Granger. 'Come and play some cards sometime, Matt. Me and Cora are always glad to see you.'

Granger looked thoughtfully at the retreating Macpherson as he headed for the Golden Nugget. Johnny Mac, he decided, knew more about what was going on than he was admitting.

'I'd better get these owlhoots over to Moses,' Billy said. 'He's gonna have a busy time.'

Granger put a hand on his arm. 'Drive the wagon back o' the office.'

Puzzled, Billy frowned. 'What we gonna do that for?'

'There's somethin' I ain't gotta handle on yet, Billy. Johnny Mac's got a tale to tell about these two in the wagon that he reckons I can't refuse to believe.'

'You mean seein' as what happened to you and Miss Amy?'

'You've got it.'

'So why'd we have to take these two critters behind the office?'

Granger slipped the knife from its strap beneath his trailcoat. He damn well wasn't going to be caught without it again. 'We're gonna cut 'em up, an' see if what I'm thinkin' is right.'

Granger stood at the tail of the wagon and looked around to make sure he wasn't being overlooked. Fortunately the stores either side were single-storeyed and around the small yard at the back of the sheriff's office was a high wooden wall. He grabbed hold of the legs of Jesse Drummond and heaved the body from the bed of the

101

wagon, stepping back as it fell to the ground.

'Jesus, Matt! I knowed these fellers were no-goods. . . .' Billy's voice tailed away as he saw Granger turn over the body and look closely at the man's back.

'What you doin' now?' Billy asked.

'No use lookin' for a slug if it went straight through him,' Granger said.

He heaved over the body until it was face up again, then tore apart the man's blood-soaked shirt, revealing beneath the dirty balbriggans equally soaked in blood. Two black holes showed where the man had been shot.

Using his knife, Granger cut away a piece of the woollen material and used it to wipe away the blood from the man's chest, revealing the entrance points of the bullets that had brought Drummond's life to an end.

Billy swallowed rapidly a couple of times, before clearing his throat noisily. 'You gonna do what I'm thinkin'?'

Granger, squatting by the body, looked up at his stepbrother. 'You gonna be OK, Billy? Maybe you wanna go inside?'

Billy shook his head furiously. 'No, no, I'm fine,' he said quickly. 'Seems I been learnin' a lot 'bout bein' a sheriff these last few weeks.' He squatted on his heels, alongside Granger. 'You seen these marks on his wrists? I'm reckonin' he's been tied up these last coupla days.'

Granger couldn't resist a smile. 'You're learnin' fast, Billy.'

He turned back to the body, and with a downward jab cut through the wall of Drummond's chest. The razor-sharp point of the knife cut through the flesh as if through candy, and Granger ripped first to the left and then to the right opening a cavity. He slowly moved the knife around until he felt the slug, levering it to force it upward through the wound.

'We got lucky, Billy. It ain't all broke up.'

He turned on his heels to wipe the slug on the ground beside him before taking the cloth he'd cut from the man's underclothing to wipe the blood from his hands.

Billy's frown grew deeper as he watched Granger. 'I sure wish I knew what you're about, Matt. I cain't see much in diggin' a slug from a feller already dead.'

Granger didn't reply. Instead, he leaned over the bed of the wagon to knock aside the derby hat from Nathan's body. Then he heaved the body out of the wagon and let it fall to the ground. As with the first body he turned it over to check that bullets had not gone straight through, then he went through the same routine as he had with the body of Drummond.

Finally, with a grunt of satisfaction, after wiping off his hands, then his knife, and lastly, the slug he'd dug from Nathan's chest, he got to his feet. He picked up the slug he'd taken from Drummond's chest and with both slugs alongside each other on his palm, he held out his hand to Billy.

'What d'you see, Billy?'

Billy shrugged. 'Coupla slugs, one mashed a bit. That's all.'

'Take another look.'

Billy frowned. 'I know what I can see. Coupla—' His mouth closed like a trap. 'Christ! They ain't the same! One's bigger!'

'You're learnin' all the time, Billy. So what you reckon we got?'

'Two guns,' said Billy promptly. 'An' Miss Cora ain't walkin' 'round with no sidearm!'

Granger nodded. These men had been killed by more than one man. Had Nathan unwittingly signed his own death warrant and that of Drummond, by telling of his last order to Ike? If that was the case, then somebody wanted both himself and Amy killed. That Macpherson was being used by Ralston was now clear. Granger had a sudden thought. Could he have it the wrong way around? Macpherson manipulating the rancher? Ralston, despite his threats out at the Lazy Y, calculated his every move. The murder of a newspaper owner, even though Ralston could distance himself from the crime, would attract lawmen from Cheyenne.

'Let's get these critters back in the wagon, an' you can take 'em over to Moses Jackson. I'm gonna have another word with Morley Roberts.'

Billy didn't move immediately. 'Matt, I got somethin' to say.' His mouth was set in a firm line. 'You got that look 'bout you I used to see in Pa. You gotta remember I'm sheriff 'round here. Folks in town are tryin' to go 'bout their business. I ain't lookin' fer gunfights down Main Street.'

Granger nodded. 'I hear you, Billy,' he said. 'You're a good man.'

Granger was leaning over the counter as he had been before being called out by Billy Haynes. Morley Roberts was again scribbling furiously into one of his books. The stubs of pencils were strewn about him, and scraps of paper littered his desk.

'I'm gonna tell you agin, I ain't goin' over all this, just so you can put it in some fancy book,' Granger said. 'I get bushwhacked, an' Billy's gonna have to sit down an' think things through. He'll have you to help him.'

'Mr Granger,' Roberts hesitated, biting his lip as if trying to find the right words for what he wanted to say. 'Could you be wrong about Macpherson?'

Granger looked at him hard. 'What you gettin' at?'

Roberts looked down at his book, his eyes scanning the words he'd written. 'There could be another explanation for the two bodies Macpherson brought in.'

'Billy's got the different slugs. Go take a look,' Granger countered.

'But suppose the odd bullet was already in Drummond's body,' Roberts said. 'He could have been walking around for months or even years with that bullet inside him. I remember when. . . .' He stopped for a moment, as if changing his mind about what he'd intended to say, before he continued, 'You know it can happen,' Roberts concluded.

'There's no arguin' with that. But I looked at the body real close afore I cut it.'

'If you don't mind my saying, Mr Granger, digging for those bullets sounds more like butchery than science. Macpherson could have been telling the truth.'

Granger smiled ruefully. 'You got too many brains for your own good, Mr Roberts.'

He turned around as the door opened behind him, and he saw a small man in a red mackinaw whom he vaguely recognized. Then he remembered the driver of the stagecoach that he'd travelled in on his journey to Springwater.

The little man touched the brim of his old cavalry hat. 'Howdy, Mr Granger. Good to see you up an' about. Last time I came through you was sick or somethin'.'

'Thanks. I'm fine.' He looked again at the man, remembering. 'It's Josh, I recall.'

The little man's face split into a grin, showing teeth blackened from chewing tobacco. 'That's me, Mr Granger! I just got in. Been back at the depot a while, missus been sick.' He pulled forward the pouch that hung on leather straps from his shoulder. 'I got some mail here for Miss Amy.'

He gave a broad wink. 'First visit, I always make. She's a lovely lady.' He looked at the bundle in his hand. 'Mostly newspaper stuff, I reckon. You gonna take it, Mr Roberts?'

The Englishman stood up from his desk and came over to the counter to take the bundle of mail from Josh. 'I'll make sure she gets it, Josh. Miss Amy's taking a couple of days off from the office.'

'Lucky lady,' Josh said. 'I'll be seein' you folks next time through.'

Again he touched the brim of his hat, this time in farewell, and started to turn towards the door when he stopped as if remembering something. He turned back to Granger.

'The letter for your pa, the Good Lord rest his soul, you got that OK?'

Granger remembered the letter that he and Amy had found out at the old homestead, now safely under lock and key in a drawer at Amy's house.

'You mean the letter came coupla months ago?'

'No, I recall that one, Mr Granger. There was another one on the stage a week after you got here.'

Granger shook his head. 'I haven't seen a letter.'

The little man screwed up his face, obviously puzzled. Then his face cleared and he snapped his fingers in triumph.

'I ain't losin' my memory, after all! The letter was addressed to Albert Granger care of his bank. Mr Fells has got it, that's for sure!' He took a sudden step back at the instant change of expressions on the faces of the two men before him. 'Have I said somethin' I shouldna done?'

CHAPTER ELEVEN

Granger and Billy Haynes stood quietly as Widow Fells, a short squat figure clad in black bombazine from head to foot, unlocked the rear door of the bank. Her stubby fingers trembled around the handle of the large key.

'I don't see why I have to do this, Sheriff,' she said. 'You'll not find a dollar missing. Folks are coming up from Cheyenne just to tell everyone their money is safe.'

'I'm sure Mr Fells left everything in order,' Billy said. 'This is nothin' to do with money. We're lookin' fer somethin' else.'

'And what could that be?' Widow Fells asked, as Billy pushed open the door to allow her to step into the bank.

'A letter for Albert Granger, my pa,' Granger said. 'We've been told it was sent in the care of your late husband.'

The woman looked up quickly at Granger, anxiety showing briefly in her eyes. 'A letter, you say? Why would poor Henry keep something like that?'

'I'll try the safe, ma'am, if I can have the key?' Billy said.

The woman reached into a fold of her voluminous skirts, and pulled out another large key. 'The money's all there. Folks don't have to get agitated,' she said.

'Yes, ma'am,' said Billy, glancing at Granger before swinging back the heavy door of the safe.

Granger could see beyond Billy the neat rows of bills, stacked inches high along the shelves of the safe. What appeared to be a small wooden tub held coins, and they made a ringing sound as Billy trickled them through his fingers checking that a letter package was not hidden beneath them.

Billy stepped back, relocked the safe door, and handed the key back to Widow Fells. 'Why don't you take a seat, ma'am? Me and Mr Granger are gonna search the rest of the bank, an' it'll take some time.'

'If you must, Sheriff.'

Widow Fells sighed heavily as she moved across the open space before the counter to sink into a cane chair. Her eyes followed the two men as they began to search the bank, her expression showing that she believed they were wasting their time.

Despite both Billy's and his own efforts, at the end of half an hour Granger was inclined to agree with her. Desks had been searched thoroughly, boxes opened, pouches examined, even accounts books had been held up by their spines in the hope that a letter package would fall from between their pages. No letter package was to be found.

'We'll not find it here, Billy,' Granger said.

Billy turned to the Widow Fells. 'I'm sorry to tell you, ma'am. We'll have to come back to your home and look there.'

Granger caught the look of dismay that briefly flickered across the woman's face. It was as if Fells's widow had expected the search to end at the bank. Was she hiding something? Or was it the normal reaction of an elderly woman to the notion of having two men turning over the homely possessions of her recently deceased husband?

'Do you really have to do that?'

Billy's voice was firm without being harsh. 'I can ride

over to the county sheriff, ma'am, an' get his OK. But if I do that, an' the letter's found, there's no tellin' what might happen.'

Again Granger saw that flicker of dismay in Widow Fells's eyes. Was the woman hiding something? She stood up, sighing deeply. 'Then you'd better look for it now,' she said.

Three hours later, in the large clapboard house of the late banker, Billy's cry of exasperation sounded around Fells's bedroom. 'We're damned wastin' our time here, Matt.' He blew air out of pursed lips. 'Are you sure the letter means so much?'

'It was important enough to be sent care of Pa's bank,' Granger pointed out. 'Sure, Fells coulda burned it or somethin', but why would he do that? We know he had the damned letter, that's for sure.' He looked around the room. 'The fact that it's missin' must mean somethin'. An' I'll wager it's tied in with that letter I found.'

Haynes looked through the window. 'I gotta go out to one of the homesteads. Feller out there reckons some critter's pouring salt on his crops. Any more homesteaders up an' leave, an' the town's gonna be in trouble.'

'I'm gonna make one last try, Billy. You wait here. I'm gonna talk alone with the widow.' Granger pulled up his mouth in a wry smile. 'An' I'm either gonna make a real jackass o' myself, or feel a real mean sonovabitch.'

Puzzled by his stepbrother's remarks, Billy watched Granger leave the room and head for the parlour. Granger tapped on the door and when invited to step in he found Widow Fells seated in a high-backed chair, embroidery on her lap. She put down her needles as Granger entered.

'Have you found the letter?'

'No, ma'am, an' that's kinda troublin',' Granger said. He watched the widow's face carefully. 'Sheriff Haynes is feelin' ornery, thinkin' he's gonna bring in the county sheriff.' Granger spoke softly and carefully.

'My pa an' Mr Fells were good friends, an' I don't want to cause lotsa trouble but if the county sheriff comes over, there's no tellin' where this will end.'

He waited a few seconds watching her closely. He wasn't feeling too proud of himself using veiled threats against a woman in mourning, but he was convinced the letter would help to answer some of the questions that remained unanswered. Widow Fells seemed to be turning over in her mind the prospect of a visit from the county sheriff. But maybe he was wrong. Would he have to go back to Billy and admit he'd made a fool of himself?

For a further minute or so she remained silent, biting her thin lips. Then finally she nodded. 'I told Henry he was being foolish, and holding on to that letter would only bring trouble. But like poor Henry, the letter's gone now.' A tear slowly ran down her lined cheek, her gaze shifting to the image of her late husband which stood in a small silver frame on a credenza. 'Am I going to be in trouble?'

'No, ma'am. You've done nothing wrong.' Granger said, relieved. 'Why d'you think your husband wanted the letter?'

She shook her head. 'I'm not sure. But he was excited and fearful at the same time. He told me that he'd make up the money we had to borrow a couple of years back.' She looked sharply at Granger. 'Oh yes, we were no different to the homesteaders or the townsfolk. We all lost money in that terrible winter.'

Granger nodded sympathetically, but his thoughts were racing. How could a letter to his father settle the debts of a man running a bank in Springwater? The more questions he tried to answer the more came hurtling his way. His father had been a small-town sheriff. He hadn't made more money than the town had paid him since he'd come back from the war.

'How did your husband think the letter would make him money?'

Widow Fells bent her head, her teeth worrying her lower lip, almost as if she was biting back the words that would answer Granger's question.

'Mrs Fells?' Granger prompted.

The woman lifted her head. 'He sold it to Mr Ralston,' she said.

Granger brought his horse out of its lope as he approached the hardpack of the town's Main Street. He planned to call at the newspaper office first, but have Roberts follow him out to Amy's if she'd stayed at home. The young man's intelligence would be useful when they thought more about what he'd learned from Widow Fells. He was now sure that there was a connection between the letter sold to Ralston and the letter he and Amy had found at the old homestead.

A deep frown marked his weather-beaten face as he gazed down Main Street. Something mighty odd was going on. Townsfolk were gathered on the street, many of them pointing up to the store fronts, the noise of their shouts, some angry, some questioning, reaching him as he passed the clapboard where Jack and Katy were living. The stage would have left a couple of hours earlier, and wasn't due back for a week. So what was prompting all the noise? Then he realized the crowd was in front of the newspaper office, and he spurred his horse forward.

He was securing the palomino to the hitching rail in front of the office, having pushed his way through the knot of people when one of the older men shouted out to him.

'Mr Granger! If Billy Haynes can't handle this town, then you gotta wear the badge like your pa!'

Granger held up his hand, acknowledging the man's remarks, but remaining silent. He went up the steps fast. Was Amy safe? That's what he needed to know. He threw open the door.

'Goddamn it to hell!' Granger roared.

In front of him the newspaper office looked as if it had been hit by a cattle stampede. Desks were overturned; papers were strewn throughout the room, signs on the walls had been torn down and lay jumbled amongst writing tablets. Overturned inkwells had splattered their contents against the rolls of unused newspaper which had been wrenched from their boxes. At the rear of the office the machinery used to produce the *Reporter* lay battered and broken as if sledge-hammers had been used to smash the printing press to pieces. Metal letters used to make up the paper were scattered across the length of the office.

From behind the counter, wrenched from its base and overturned, someone groaned. Granger was behind the counter in an instant, squatting by the fallen figure of Morley Roberts. Blood poured from the side of the young man's head. Roberts struggled to sit up, his hand to his head, blood trickling over his knuckles.

'Matthew! Thank God you're here!'

'Amy! Where's Amy?'

Roberts shook his head, causing him to wince. 'She must be still at home. She didn't come to the office.'

Relief surged through Granger's body. 'Who was it? Who did this?'

'Three of them, wearing masks. They didn't give me a

chance, charging through the door while I was writing at my desk.'

'Were they tall, short, what were they wearing?'

'It happened so quickly. Wait a moment!' A gleam came into Roberts's eyes. 'The leader. He had a mark, maybe a tattoo, on the back of his hand.'

Granger's mind went back over his days in Springwater. Where had he seen such a mark on a man's hand? Then he remembered, and he cursed loudly. 'I know the sonovabitch! He'd not do something like this without orders.'

Granger reached out to grasp Roberts's head, turning the young man's head towards him. 'Scalp wound,' he said. 'They bleed like hell, but you'll be OK.'

He stood up, putting his arm out to help Roberts to his feet, before going across the office to reach into the small cupboard where a pitcher and jug of water sat on a table. He soaked a cloth in water, and returned to Roberts.

'Clean yourself up,' he said, handing the cloth to Roberts.

Not waiting for Roberts's answer he swung on his heel, and again crossed the office to open a dusty cupboard in the corner of the office.

'I didn't know Miss Amy keeps that!' A surprised Roberts stared at the scatter-gun Granger had taken from the cupboard.

'She doesn't, an' don't you go lettin' on, or she'll be mad at me,' Granger said shortly. 'I put it here a few days ago.' He bit his lip, angry with himself. 'Only I was expectin' to be here for anythin' like this.'

He looked around the office surveying the damage. 'How much you reckon this is gonna cost to put right?'

Roberts looked around the office, calculating, before giving a deep sigh of frustration. 'Damn it all, Matthew! You're talking maybe seven hundred and fifty dollars.' He paused a second. 'Then there's the loss of income while we can't get the paper out, and transport costs. New machinery will have to come from Cheyenne, maybe even further.'

Granger nodded abruptly. He held the scatter-gun in one hand while easing his Navy in its holster.

'What are you planning to do, Matthew?'

Granger pulled his lips back from his teeth in a grin that didn't reach his eyes. 'I'm gonna get that money for Amy. That's what I'm gonna do!'

Granger was twenty yards from the Golden Nugget, walking plumb down the centre of Main Street when he saw Cora rush down the steps from the boardwalk, and hurry towards him. She held her hands above her head, her palms turned towards him.

'Don't Matt, please don't!' Cora cried out.

'Is Macpherson there?' Granger asked brusquely as she reached him.

'He's out at the Lazy Y.'

Her hand went past the scatter-gun held high by Granger to take hold of his shoulder. 'Please Matt, please! Don't do this! You'll start a war, an' God knows where it'll end.'

'Get outa the way, Cora!' He moved to shove her aside, then appeared to change his mind, and grabbed her roughly by the arm. 'No, you're comin' along. I'm gonna need you.'

Ignoring her cries of protest, he dragged her alongside him, her feet sliding along the street as she desperately fought to stay upright. He mounted the steps and pushed through the batwing doors of the Nugget. As he stepped forward into the big room, he shoved Cora away from him, sending her crashing into chairs, spilling them to the ground. Alarmed at the noise, men turned from the tables to look in the direction of the doorway. Granger held the scatter-gun high.

'Any good honest folks wanna leave, do it now!' Granger shouted.

There was a surge of men scrambling away from their seats, some rushing through a back door that led to an alleyway, some rushing past him to scamper through the batwing doors.

From the corner of his eye Granger saw the Mexican barkeep reach below the counter. Granger swung around and fired off one of the barrels, the shot blasting the glass mirror at the back of the bar, sending the Mexican running along the bar beneath flying glass to disappear through a door.

Granger looked at the three men at the table over to his right. They hadn't moved. Coins sat among bottles and glasses in front of them. Each of the men sat watching him, ignoring their cards, their arms hanging loosely against their sides.

'Sheriff Haynes gonna throw you in jail, he gets back,' called Zack Rudman who sat on the far side of the table from Granger. 'You comin' in here, shootin' off that scatter-gun.' He looked at his two companions, and snickered. 'We're a law-abidin' town, Mr Granger.'

Granger raised the barrel of the scatter-gun, spun on his heel, and blasted the chandelier that hung from the centre of the room. Splintered glass flew in all directions, the chandelier swinging wildly on its rope.

'Matt, have you lost your mind?' Cora screamed.

'Go upstairs to that office of yourn, an' bring me a thousand dollars,' he ordered her, keeping his eyes on the men around the table.

'Now I know you're crazy!'

Granger drew his Navy, turned towards the bar, and fired. The mirror at the end of the bar, previously untouched by the scatter-gun, exploded in a storm of glass shards as the heavy slug hit home.

Granger swung back to the table, his Navy held high at arm's length and Zack froze, half out of his chair. His hand, with its tattoo above his knuckles, was an inch from the butt of his sidearm.

'Go get the money, Cora! Or I really get to work!'

'You sonovabitch, Matthew Granger,' Cora screamed. 'You're no different from your brother Charlie! Your pa shoulda kept you here back then for Johnny Mac to kill!'

'Go get the money!'

He stepped forward to the table. 'On your feet, Rudman!'

'An' if I don't?'

'You're forgettin' somethin'. I'm still a sworn deputy.' His lips curled back from his teeth. 'I'm arrestin' you for breaking up the *Reporter*. You resist arrest an' I'll shoot you down.'

Zack must have given a signal. The man to Granger's right came out of his chair fast. But not fast enough. Granger brought the barrel of his Navy round to sideswipe the man. Blood gushed from a broken nose. He fell back like a sack of corn.

Zack had his sidearm halfway out its holster when Granger rammed the barrel of his Navy against Zack's forehead. There was a metallic click of the sidearm being cocked.

'This other feller gonna try somethin'?' Granger asked quietly.

Zack's face turned ashen, beads of sweat beginning to form on his temples. 'Don't make a move, Fletcher!' Moving very slowly he let his sidearm fall back into its holster.

116

'I ain't doin' nothing!' Fletcher exclaimed. 'What the hell's all this about?'

Granger stood back a pace, his Navy still held at arm's length, aiming at Zack's head.

'You both stand up, an' drop your gunbelts real slow. You make a wrong move an' I'll kill you.'

'For Chris'sakes, mister! I came in here fer a game o' cards,' Fletcher said, his fingers scrabbling at the buckle of his gunbelt. 'I ain't tanglin' with no lawman!'

'Then you shoulda left when you had the chance,' Granger said. He looked down at the man on the floor who was beginning to stir. 'Take off his gunbelt an' wake him up,' he ordered Fletcher. 'You're gonna carry the belts down to the jailhouse. Do as you're told, an' you can ride outa town.'

'Sure, mister! Whatever you say!'

Over to his right, Cora came down the stairs, a packet in her hand, her anxious eyes surveying the group of men around the table. She reached the bottom of the stairs and hesitated.

'Bring the money over here,' Granger said. He tossed the empty scatter-gun to Fletcher and held out his left hand, his right still holding his Navy aimed at the three men, now all on their feet.

'Johnny Mac'll kill you for this,' she said, holding up the package.

'An' I'm gonna help 'im!' Zack spat out.

Granger ignored him, taking the package without looking in Cora's direction. He gestured with the barrel of his Navy at the three men.

'Down to the jailhouse,' he ordered. 'An' I find you been lyin' to me, Fletcher, I'll make you damned sorry!'

CHAPTER TWELVE

Amy Morgan surveyed the stack of currency bills lined up along the top of the counter, now upright after Roberts's valiant efforts to bring some order back to the offices of the *Reporter*.

'Matthew, I can't take this money,' she said.

Granger swung around from his conversation with Roberts. 'What did you say?'

'This money is not ours, Matthew. It belongs to the Golden Nugget and John Macpherson.'

'Zack Rudman wouldn't move an inch without being told, an' he's Johnny Mac's man.' Granger said. 'Morley's given sworn testimony an' Billy's keepin' Rudman an' that other no-good in jail for Judge Parker. I'll catch up with the third no-good in time.'

'But it doesn't change anything about the money,' Amy countered. 'When Judge Parker gets here next month I'll take it up with him. I'll explain to him what happened and he'll give his judgement.'

'An' then maybe another coupla months go by without you gettin' the paper out,' said Granger sharply. 'Take the money, an' Morley can get down to Cheyenne an' start fixin' a new press.'

Amy shook her head, and was about to speak when the door was thrown open and the three turned towards the door to see Cora standing on the threshold. Her face was pale, and her hand on the doorpost was trembling. Her breathing was short as if she had been running.

'Johnny Mac an' three of Ralston's gunmen are riding into town,' she gasped. 'They mean to bust out Zack Rudman!'

'Does Billy know this?' Granger rapped out.

'I've just told him,' she said. She turned to close the door and leave when she was halted by Amy calling out her name.

'Cora! You must take this back.' Amy came from behind the counter to push into Cora's hand the package of currency bills she'd scooped up from the counter. Cora looked for a second at Granger. Then, without another word, she stepped out on to the boardwalk, and closed the door behind her.

'That's darned strange,' Granger said slowly. 'Now why d'you think she's warnin' us after all that business at the Nugget?'

Amy whirled to face him, her face pink. 'Sometimes, Matthew Granger,' she snapped angrily, 'you show little sense!'

Before a surprised Granger could respond the door was thrown open again, and Billy Haynes burst into the office. 'You heard what's happenin', Matt? Johnny Mac's gone crazy!' He looked anxiously at the three faces turned in his direction. 'I'm gonna have to talk to him.'

'You think talkin's gonna be good enough?'

Billy looked at Granger, his shoulders drooping an inch. 'No,' he said finally.

'We go out together an' face 'em,' said Granger grimly. 'How long we got?'

'Twenty minutes maybe,' Billy said.

'I'm coming out with you,' Roberts said.

Granger turned. 'You're a writer, Mr Roberts. The street's no place for you.'

The Englishman stood up. 'Three years in the British Army, 89th Regiment under Major A. H. Mercer,' he said flatly. 'Is that good enough?'

Granger grinned, and held up his hand, palm outward, in mock surrender. 'I shoulda guessed that first day on the stage, Mr Roberts. OK, get a long gun from Billy. Put yourself on top of the dry goods store. Any o' those no-goods try to bushwhack us from an alleyway, you shoot him down.' He looked carefully at Roberts. 'You ever killed a man?'

The look in the Englishman's eyes told him all he needed to know and he turned back to Billy. His step-brother's new Navy would make it easier for what he was planning.

'Get as much thirty-six as you can. Put some boxes inside the door of the livery stable in case we have to fall back down the street.'

He faced the two men. 'You easy with all that?'

The two men nodded, and moved quickly to go out of the door. Granger went to the cupboard and took out the scatter-gun he'd hidden away. As he broke the gun and pushed in shells, he became aware that Amy's eyes were following his every move.

'Matthew,' she said, and he lifted his head to look straight into her eyes.

'Please, please, don't go out there. Please stop this now. Go back to Boston.' She took a deep breath and spoke quickly, the words tumbling over each other, 'I'll come with you if you want me.' Her head went down but not before her face had turned pink. A tear fell from her cheek to the floor. 'I can't lose you now.'

Granger stood still, breathing deeply and slowly.

'An' what about Billy?' he said finally. 'Do I leave him alone to face what's comin' his way?' He put his hand gently beneath her chin and raised her head. 'An' Pa bein' killed, an' all the hard times he an' your father went through tryin' to stop Ralston, an' Henry Fells driven to hang himself or maybe murdered, an' Jack an' Katy an' other homesteaders driven outa their homes? Macpherson is Ralston's man, we know that now. I can't walk away from all o' this.' He leaned the scatter-gun against the counter, and put both his hands on her shoulders. 'How could we ever be happy?'

She looked directly at him for a few seconds. Then she turned away, stifling a sob. 'I pray to God you'll be safe.'

Granger picked up the scatter-gun and without looking again in Amy's direction, he walked across to the door and stepped out on to the boardwalk.

Granger and Billy stood shoulder to shoulder in the middle of Main Street. The boardwalks either side of them were deserted, although Granger had caught sight of faces in the upper floors of the one or two buildings that boasted such a luxury.

Before taking up his position he'd glanced up at Walter Rogers's dry goods store. Roberts must have seen him look up, as he showed himself for an instant reassuring Granger he was in position. Not for the first time Granger was glad to have the Englishman alongside him. He just hoped Roberts was as good with a long gun as he was with a pen. If he and Billy were killed would Roberts write about them in some fancy book? He thrust the crazy thought aside as he saw the cloud of dust kicked up by riders approaching the end of Main Street.

'OK, Billy,' he said. 'Here they come.'

As instructed by Granger, Billy moved several paces to

his right while Granger moved to his left. He looked over to the alleyway on his right and maybe twenty yards down the street. If there was an attempt to bushwhack them, that's where the shots would come from.

'They gonna try an' ride us down?' Billy called.

'I guess not. Johnny Mac will mebbe try an' talk,' called back Granger.

As he spoke, the three men advancing down Main Street with Macpherson in the middle, reined in their horses to a walk. Twenty yards closer to where Billy and Granger stood, the three men halted in front of the Chinaman's eating-house. Granger watched as they slid from their saddles to secure the animals at the hitching rail. Then they turned to face down Main Street in the direction of Granger and Billy. The two men flanking Macpherson hitched up their gunbelts while Macpherson shrugged back his Prince Albert coat to reveal his pearl handled .44 Smith & Wesson.

Macpherson glanced briefly either side of him as if checking that the other two were with him, before the three men slowly began to advance down the street until they were maybe twenty feet away from Granger and Billy.

'You shot up my saloon, Matt.' Macpherson called. 'We're gonna have to settle that.' He looked across at Billy who was standing, legs apart, his gun hand resting easily down the side of his body. 'You got no right to hold Zack, Billy! You gotta have evidence to hold a man in jail. Judge Parker ain't gonna like it.'

'I'll take my chances with the judge,' Billy replied.

'That ain't good enough, Billy! I want Zack outa jail, an' I mean to get him out.'

'That's agin the law, an' you know it,' Billy called.

There was a snicker of harsh laughter from one of the men alongside Macpherson. He was unshaven, a battered hat pulled low on his head, a red bandanna around the weathered flesh of his neck. 'What the hell we waitin' for?'

'You're crossin' the line, Johnny Mac,' called Granger. 'You're gonna end up breakin' rocks down in Cheyenne.'

He saw the movement of colour in the corner of his eye as someone moved at the entrance to the alleyway down the street. Almost instantly there came the crack of a long gun closely followed by a scream of pain.

From out of the alleyway staggered a man, blood gushing from the upper part of his arm. His yells of pain bounced around the street between the buildings. On legs which appeared to barely support his weight he tottered a few yards before falling to the ground, twisting as he fell to push his back against the edge of the boardwalk. He tore off his bandanna with a grimy hand, and attempted to stem the flow of blood dripping onto the hardpack.

'You bushwhackin' now, Johnny Mac?' Granger called, his scatter-gun resting easily in his grasp, his eyes never leaving Macpherson's hand close to the pearl-handled butt.

The gunman to the left of Macpherson shouted a wild curse, his hand dropping to the butt of his sidearm. The weapon was barely an inch out of its holster when the man was hurtled back several feet by the .36 slug that hit him full in the chest, driving him down to the hardpack. He lay still, his face to the sky, legs apart. The sound of Billy's gunshot reverberated around the buildings either side of Main Street.

The four men left standing froze as if in a tableau. Granger heard the gunman standing alongside Macpherson mutter something and then take a pace back.

'Guess I was lookin' at the wrong man,' Macpherson said evenly. He brushed his coat, allowing it to fall over his sidearm. 'This ain't finished, Matt, you know that,' he said.

'Springwater woulda been better for you not comin' back.'

'You threw in with Ralston an' all his plans,' Granger said. 'I ain't forgettin' that.'

Granger remained watching as the saloon owner turned without a further word and retreated down Main Street. The gunman left standing, his hands held clear of his gunbelt, stepped across to drag the dead man along the ground. Clutching his arm, still moaning with pain, the third man staggered behind them.

Granger glanced across at his stepbrother. Billy was standing side-on to the length of Main Street, his arm extended, his sidearm aiming at the retreating men.

CHAPTER THIRTEEN

Granger left the barbershop, running his fingers over his freshly shaved chin, and walked down the steps to cross Main Street. He could see Billy waiting for him at the entrance to the Majestic.

A couple of townsfolk passing in a buggy called a cheerful greeting to him as he crossed the street. Springwater sure was a change from Boston, he thought. There, walking across the street was becoming a life and death adventure with horse-drawn trams hurtling along, their drivers not caring who got in their way. Maybe when his life got quieter back East he'd come back to Springwater again when the Ralstons and the Macphersons were no longer around. Unless, of course, it turned out that they were still around and he wasn't. He reached Billy as a townsman was just parting company from his stepbrother.

'Folks reckon you're doin' a fine job, Sheriff,' the townsman said. He turned, as Granger joined them. 'That Ralston feller's maybe not goin' to take over this town after all.' He put a finger to his hat and walked away.

'Mebbe the councilmen are gonna pay you more,' Granger said, as they entered the hotel.

Billy grinned and shook his head. 'They wanna talk to both of us, that's all I know.'

Granger saw that the same desk clerk who had first

drawn his attention to the *Reporter* was manning the desk.

'Howdy, Mr Granger, Sheriff Haynes,' Willy greeted them cheerfully, taking their gunbelts and carefully hanging them on the wooden pegs behind him. 'Councilmen are in the big parlour down the hall, second door on the right.'

Granger remembered the room from his brief stay at the hotel when he'd arrived in the stage. He led Billy along the corridor and opened the door. As the two men stepped in, half-a-dozen men rose from their chairs.

Granger recognized Reverend Dunning from the stage-coach but the others were strangers to him. What was all this about? There'd been lots of talk about the confrontation with Macpherson, and he guessed that some might be unhappy about a shooting in Main Street. He supposed that if he'd been running a store in town he'd be tempted to feel the same. But if these men settled for a quiet life then Ralston would be ordering them around before the year was out.

He guessed that some might even still favour Macpherson as sheriff over Billy. Surely they realized that the shootout was the result of the attack on the offices of the *Reporter*? Zack Rudman and a couple of others might have wrecked the office but it was Macpherson who gave the order to Rudman, of that he was convinced.

It was Dunning who stepped forward to greet them and shake each man warmly by the hand. 'Take your seats, gentlemen, and thank you both for coming to talk with us.'

Granger saw that two chairs were placed facing the semicircle of chairs occupied by the councilmen. Was this intended to be some sort of interrogation? Maybe the warm welcome from Dunning ruled out being asked to quit town, but it was obvious that these men were looking for answers.

'What can we do for you gentlemen?' Granger asked, as he and Billy took their seats.

Dunning nodded to a small red-faced man who sported a fancy blue vest beneath his dark blue Prince Albert. A heavy gold watch chain decorating his ample middle jiggled on his vest as he cleared his throat noisily.

'Joseph Barrow's my name, Mr Granger,' he said finally. 'I can use fancy words if needs be, but I know you Grangers prefer hard talking.' There was a ripple of supporting noise from the other men. 'Until that raid on the bank a couple of months back, this town was quietly getting on with its business.'

Granger remained silent. There was little to gain at this point in reminding Barrow that the town had remained quiet because Pa and Amy's father had ensured that Ralston's actions to take over the town were kept under control.

'Don't forget, Joe, the store-keepers who've quit,' said a broad-shouldered man wearing a leather jacket.

'An' there was that bad business with the young gal gettin' attacked by one of Ralston's no-goods,' said another.

'I'm not saying that it's all been perfect,' Barrow said. 'Damnit all—' He broke off to glance at Dunning. 'Sorry, Reverend. Excuse my language. All I'm saying is,' he continued, 'we've been quiet around these parts for a long while, and it's good for the sawmill business if the town stays quiet. Lots of folk around here have good jobs there.'

He looked around at his fellow councilmen, before staring hard at Granger. 'Gunfights in Main Street and folks shooting up the saloon ain't getting us anywhere.' He grunted with apparent exasperation. 'I've seen more dead men these last weeks than I saw in the old frontier days.'

Barrow leaned back in his chair, again looking around

at his fellow councilmen, maybe hoping to see some expressions of support.

'That's all I want to say for the moment, Reverend,' he said.

'Thank you for that, Joseph,' said Dunning. He looked at Granger and Billy. 'Do you wish to say anything?'

Granger was about to speak when a knock sounded at the door. One of the councilmen stood up to open it. 'What is it, Mr Jackson? We're in a meeting here.'

The town's undertaker stood on the threshold, peering through half-moon glasses into the room. He looked, and sounded, agitated. 'You got Sheriff Haynes with you? I gotta show him somethin' quick.'

Billy got up from his chair. 'I'm here, Moses. What's goin' on?'

'I need you 'cross the street, Sheriff. I'll tell you there.'

Billy raised enquiring eyebrows in the direction of Granger before turning to Dunning. 'Maybe I'd better see what Moses wants, Reverend. Will you wait, or can Mr Granger answer any questions?'

Dunning turned to his fellow councilmen, and seeing their nods, turned back to Billy 'I'm sure Mr Granger can help us, Sheriff.'

Billy picked up his hat from the floor beside his chair, and nodded to the semi-circle of men. 'Good day, gentlemen,' he said.

As soon as the door had closed behind Billy and Jackson, Granger spoke. 'Let's get somethin' clear. I ain't here to take the job away from Billy. Ralston may have fixed it so Billy got the badge, but I reckon Ralston's regrettin' he did that. Billy's doin' a good job, an' he's learnin' fast. He's part of my family an' I'm just givin' him a hand. Anyways, I'll be goin' back East as soon as this trouble's cleared up.'

The councilmen exchanged looks with each other, a couple shrugging their shoulders as if dismissing any notion they had of asking Granger to follow his father in the office of sheriff.

Dunning spoke again. 'We all agreed you should hear from Mr Barrow first. There are many folks in town who agree with him.'

'Yeah, Reverend,' said the man in the leather jacket. 'An' there's plenty of folks who don't.' He shifted in his seat to face Granger. 'Henry Walker's my name, Mr Granger, an' I ain't denyin that Ralston brought peace 'round this town in the early days. Then we were lucky to have your father as sheriff.' Walker breathed in heavily. 'But since the bad winter Ralston's been tryin' to take over this town. And we all know homesteaders hereabouts who've upped an' quit.'

Walker frowned. 'Since the raid on the bank lotsa things been goin' on in this town. I know you all think I'm crazy for thinkin' like this but I just gotta feelin' that everythin's maybe connected, an' Ralston's involved.'

'That's nonsense, Henry!' Barrow exclaimed. 'What could Ralston possibly gain?'

'The death of my pa for a start,' Granger said quietly.

The half-a-dozen men stared at him, some with puzzled frowns, a couple clearly about to object to Granger's claim. Granger stood up. Sitting on that damn chair made him feel as if he were asking for a job. He looked around at the councilmen, his glance resting briefly on each face.

'Ralston knew as long as my pa was alive, he'd always have someone tryin' to stop him takin' over this town. Maybe without his support Mrs Morgan wouldn't have carried on her father's work'

'Hold on, Mr Granger,' Barrow said. 'Albert Granger was killed by those no-goods who tried to rob the bank.'

Granger looked straight at Barrow. 'The whole town knew that Pa took his coffee with Walter Rogers. Just suppose that Ralston had three of his no-goods rob the bank but have them fire a shot knowin' that Pa would try an' stop them. I'm supposin' Ralston told 'em they could keep the money, but their real job was to kill my pa.'

'That's a lot of supposin',' said a grey-bearded man.

'But the plan went wrong when Macpherson appeared,' objected a tall man in a dark city suit.

Granger shook his head. 'Everythin' happened as Ralston planned. He wasn't gonna risk being connected with the murder by three no-goods.'

Henry Walker came halfway out his chair. 'I got it, Mr Granger! So Ralston had Macpherson kill any man Albert Granger didn't get!'

'I say again,' Barrow said. 'This is nonsense!'

'Go an' look at the bank clock,' Granger said. 'A shot was fired to bring out my pa. What the no-goods didn't know was that it also brought out Macpherson who'd checked his timepiece with that clock in the morning.'

The Reverend Denning was frowning, obviously marshalling his thoughts before he posed his question. 'But, Mr Granger, how could the attack on the stage be connected to an earlier bank raid?'

'You remember the two owlhoots, Reverend, an' what one of 'em said?' Granger said. 'They were after the mail bag.'

'That's mighty strange,' Barrow said. 'Anything really valuable from Cheyenne or the stage stations comes separately by armed guard.'

'I only learned that a coupla days ago, Mr Barrow,' Granger said. 'I reckon those no-goods were lookin' for a letter addressed to my pa.'

He held up his hand as several of the councilmen

began to ask questions at the same time. 'No, I don't know why,' he said. 'I've seen one letter addressed to my pa, an' I can't make much sense of it.'

His glance swept over the men before him. 'I believe my pa found out somethin' that Ralston wants to keep secret. Somethin' that would destroy Ralston. I do know that Henry Fells took another letter addressed to my pa an' sold it to Ralston. But I don't know what was in the letter.'

Barrow turned to his fellow councilman. 'OK, Henry, it looks as if I got this one wrong. I'm not convinced that Mr Granger's right on everything but something's going on, that's plain.'

'That's mighty generous of you, Joe,' Walker said. He gave a wry smile before his next words. 'But there's still somethin' that makes no sense to me.' He looked towards Granger. 'Ralston's been keepin' a bunch o' gunslingers out at the Lazy Y for as long as I remember. Now in a few weeks six of 'em are dead.'

'Seven,' Granger said. 'I killed one in the woods nor'east of the town.'

There was a sharp intake of breath from all the councilmen. Granger moved from behind the chair where he'd been standing to take a position close to them. He looked down at the seated men, resting for a few moments on each of their faces.

'Ralston's been ready to let seven of his men die. The three at the bank he deliberately set up for killin'. What does that tell you?'

Joseph Barrow was the first to speak. 'He's playing for very high stakes, indeed,' he said thoughtfully. 'But what could they be?'

'I reckon we're gonna soon find out,' Granger said. 'Good day, gentlemen.'

*

Amy was watching Granger place the scatter-gun in the cupboard at the rear of the newspaper office.

'I'll get some shells from Walter later,' he said. 'Better we're ready.'

'Surely, they'll not come back, Matt, now that the paper has been closed down,' Amy said.

'No point in takin' chances,' Granger said. 'When those fellers from Cheyenne arrive to check Fells's bank they'll have my money from Boston. You'll soon be back in business.'

'Matt! You can't just give me your money!'

Granger's face was split with a large grin. 'I ain't givin' it to you, Amy, I'm investin' in a fine business.'

Amy laughed, but then her expression changed. 'That's if Ralston doesn't get his way,' she said soberly. 'I wish we knew what he was planning.'

'Surely it must be something to do with bringing his cattle eastwards where they can ford the river,' Roberts said. 'He's driven off the homesteaders who would have barred his way. Once he controls the town he'll have a clear route to the east.'

'But the railhead is to the south of the Lazy Y,' objected Amy. 'We've thought of this before.'

'Mebbe we haven't studied on this enough,' Granger said slowly. He closed the cupboard door on the scatter-gun and turned to face Amy.

'What land is to the east of here?'

'A huge ranch owned by a company in London. An English Lord by the name of Moreton Frewen runs the spread.'

'Frewen did you say?' Roberts exclaimed. 'I know him! We were at Cambridge together! That's a university in England,' he added by way of explanation.

'Morley, you sure take some beatin'!' Granger

exclaimed. He thought quickly, reaching a decision. 'Tomorrow, you ride over an' poke 'round. Have a word with your English friend. Mebbe Ralston's aimin' at somehow joinin' up with him.' He paused, a look of puzzlement on his face. 'But what's forcin' Ralston to move so fast he's ready to sacrifice half-a-dozen of his men?'

He turned as the door from the street opened and Billy Haynes stepped into the office. 'Heck, Billy! You look as if you've just met a ghost!'

Billy was white-faced, and the green tinge of his face showed that whatever he'd eaten that day was no longer with him. He looked down at his hands, as if finding it difficult to believe what he was seeing.

'Reckon I musta washed twenty times this last hour,' he said.

Roberts pushed a chair forward. 'Come and sit down, Sheriff.'

'Yeah, think I will,' Billy crossed the room, and slumped down in the chair.

'What's been happenin' that you're all cut up like this?' Granger asked.

Billy took a deep breath. 'Homesteader north of the town was over by the river. He came across two bodies, an' brought 'em into Moses.' Billy shot a look in Amy's direction. 'They weren't too fresh,' he said, his mouth twisting. 'Matt, those two bodies you an' Miss Amy saw! They gotta be the same!'

Granger knew that Billy had taken Moses Jackson and a cart out to the place where he and Amy had seen the bodies. Nothing was found, and it was assumed that wild animals had dragged the bodies away. But who had Nathan and Jesse Drummond told about the two bodies? Somebody had moved them, that was plain.

'They looked as if they'd been religious folk, an' I told

Moses they had to be given a proper burial,' Billy continued. He swallowed a couple of times. 'That meant gettin'
their clothes off 'em.'

'I'm sure their folks would have wanted it that way,'
Amy said quietly.

'Anyways, it's done now,' said Billy. 'An' it's all for the
best, 'cos I got somethin' to show you all.' He dug into his
pocket and pulled out a letter package. 'What do you
make of this? I found it in a secret pocket in the coat of
one of those poor critters.'

Billy stood up and spread out the letter on the nearest
desk. Bold print stated that the letter came from the
Indian Bureau in Washington. Official language ordered
the bearers of the letter to investigate with Albert Edward
Granger of Springwater, Wyoming, the matters on which
the carrier of the letter had been briefed. The letter was
signed by General Ely Parker.

For a full minute there was absolute silence in the
room. Then Granger spoke. 'This has gotta be somethin'
to do with the Lazy Y! The high stakes Ralston's been
playin' for!' His clenched fist thudded into the palm of his
other hand. 'The letter Fells sold to Ralston musta been a
letter from this General to Pa tellin' him these men were
on their way.'

'But what about that letter we found at the homestead?'
Amy asked.

Granger shrugged. 'Mebbe it was Pa playin' a sorta
game after all.'

'No, wait!' Roberts exclaimed. 'I think I have it!' He
paced up and down the office, clicking his fingers, clearly
trying to jog his memory. He stopped suddenly and
whirled around to face them. 'I've got it! Ely Parker is the
name Donehogawa of the Iroquois took when he joined
the US Army!'

He smacked his hand against his brow in frustration. 'There was something about General Parker being specially appointed by President Grant.' Roberts's face fell. 'That's all I can remember,' he said, grabbing a pencil from his desk. He scribbled a note before thrusting his book into a high pocket on his new coat.

Granger was staring, amazed, at Roberts. 'How in tarnation did you even know that?'

'I read about him in a newspaper in New York,' said Roberts cheerfully. 'I had to use it as bedclothes once.'

'Morley, I reckon you've earned a bonus—'

His final words were drowned as the street window of the *Reporter* exploded. Shards of glass scythed high through the air as Amy's screams of fear were matched by the shouts of shock and fury from the three men.

CHAPTER FOURTEEN

'Get down! Get down!' Granger yelled.

He flung himself across the room to clutch Amy around the waist, dragging her to the floor. They landed in a tangled heap, his spurs ripping into her long skirt. Ignoring her cries, he threw himself across her body, vaguely aware that behind him Roberts and Billy had also thrown themselves to the boards. For a second only the heavy breathing of the four could be heard as they waited, Granger feeling his muscles knot in his stomach. He knew what was coming next.

Then it began.

In a stream of horrendous noise, bullets from sidearms and long guns smashed through what remained of the street window, hammering into the wall. Lethal splinters of wood and chips of rough plaster flew through the air. Paper signs, only recently replaced by Roberts, were ripped to pieces and scraps of paper sent flying to the ceiling before they swirled to the floor like leaves falling from trees in the autumn. Metal whined against metal only inches away from Granger and Amy.

Roberts and Billy, faces pressed hard against the boards of the floor, held their hands against their ears. Amy, who lay on her back beneath Granger, had her head turned away from him. Her eyes were screwed shut, fear obscuring the softness of her features. Beneath the never-ending thrum and whip-like cracks of bullets, Granger could hear Billy swearing in a harsh monotone.

There was a pause in the firing, and Granger looked down at Amy who turned her head to look up at him, her eyes wide, her lips trembling, her face chalk-white. Granger cautiously raised his head to look around the office. They'd all been saved by the smashed up printing press, he realized. In his attempts to bring some order back to the office after the no-goods had brought in their hammers, Roberts had lined up the ruined metal below the office window awaiting collection by Sam Bryce. The metal plates had provided a life-saving shield.

There was a shout from across the street.

'I warned you, Granger!'

'That's Ralston,' Granger said softly.

Without shifting from Amy, he reached back to slide his Navy from its holster. Without taking aim, but pointing somewhere in the direction from which the voice came, he let off two quick shots. If anyone had meant to rush the office, they'd now be having second thoughts.

Granger spoke in a low tone, 'Billy. Morley. You two OK?'

Hearing both men reply, Granger rolled away from Amy and crawled on his belly across to the cupboard for the scatter-gun he'd placed there earlier. The door to the cupboard was shot full of holes and his heart missed a beat until he realized that the weapon was below the level of the metal plates of the old printing press.

He pulled open the door. Two damn shells, then the scatter-gun would be useless. If only he'd gone across to Walter Rogers for more shells earlier in the day. He shifted like

Roberts to support himself on one knee. Billy, too, scrambled from the boards into a similar position. Amy stayed down, but propped herself on one elbow. Granger looked at her, and then turned towards what remained of the window.

'Ralston! We got Mrs Morgan with us,' he called. 'Let her walk outa here, an' I give you my word we'll not shoot until she's clear.'

'She's thrown in with you, Granger! Now she has to pay the price!'

Granger swore beneath his breath. 'Ralston musta gone crazy!'

'Mr Ralston, this is Sheriff Haynes!' Billy shouted. 'You kill just one of us in here, an' they'll hang you down in Cheyenne for murder! You really want that?'

There was a pause. Hell! Granger swept out his arms sending himself and the other two men to the boards as once more bullets flew through the office, smashing into the wooden walls, flinging books and packs of paper hurtling across the room. Metal screamed as slugs hit the stove pipe in the corner and ricocheted around the room. Had any one in the room been standing up they would have been felled in an instant.

'That enough answer for you, Billy?'

'That's Johnny Mac,' Granger exclaimed.

Billy thrust his Navy above the metal plate and fired, the blast ringing in the ears of all four. Billy ducked down again.

'How many you reckon?'

'Six, maybe seven,' Granger said grimly. 'Macpherson bein' with 'em changes things. He ain't gonna be talkin' any more.' Granger turned to Amy. 'Is there any other way out of here?'

Amy shook her head. 'The only door is the one to the street.'

138

Granger dismissed the door from his thoughts immediately. With six maybe more guns across the street if anyone of them tried to run for it, even with covering fire, he'd be cut down before he'd made two yards.

'Wait a moment!' Amy exclaimed. 'There's a trapdoor!'

She pointed behind her into the corner of the room. 'Underneath the old rug! It's just big enough to get through.'

'I got one in my office,' Billy said. 'Fellers who built these places put 'em there so they could get down to check out the timbers.'

It was too quiet, Granger suddenly realized. He picked up the scatter-gun, gestured to the others and blasted across the street without taking aim. There was a scream of pain, and the soft thud of a man falling. The sound came from only a few feet away.

'Christ!' Billy exclaimed. 'He musta been creepin' up on us.'

Granger swallowed hard. He'd just gotten lucky and he knew it. Next time all their luck might run out. He swung around to face Roberts.

'You got anythin' put away that might help?'

In answer to the question Roberts crawled across to the leather bag by the splintered desk that he'd sat at since taking up the job offer from Amy Morgan. He crawled back and unbuckled the bag.

'It's not much,' he said, taking out the .41 calibre rimfire pistol and offering it to Granger.

Granger waved it aside. 'Keep it.' He looked hard at Roberts. 'You're gonna take Amy down that trapdoor an' get away beneath the stores. Me an' Billy here will give coverin' fire.'

Roberts's expression hardened, and he shook his head. 'Miss Amy goes,' he said. 'But I stay. Or we all go.'

'We all go, an' Ralston or Johnny Mac will guess what's happenin'. Me an' Billy are gonna keep their minds on this place.'

Roberts opened his mouth to object once more, and Granger held up his hand. 'Morley, you were a soldier.' His mouth twisted. 'I wore a captain's bars a while back. You're outranked.'

He turned to Amy without giving Roberts a chance to say any more.

'Amy, you get across to the corner. Make sure you keep your head down. When Morley opens the trapdoor, you get down there darned quick. Me an' Billy ain't carryin' that much we can keep on firin' 'cross the street.'

'Matt,' she said. Her fingers stretched out towards him, searching for his hand. He took her hand in his, looking directly into her eyes for a second. Then he pushed away her hand and nodded to Roberts. He turned away as Roberts and Amy, bent low, scuttled across the office.

A few minutes later, Granger and Billy were ready, kneeling about six feet apart, facing the street, their sidearms resting on the top of the metal plates propped against the wall below the window. Granger turned his head to look behind him. Roberts had opened the lid of the trapdoor, made of sturdy oak. By good fortune, the raised door faced the street, and would offer Roberts and Amy sufficient protection if shooting broke out again from the other side of the street.

'Go now!' Granger ordered.

He paused, and then at his nod, he and Billy fired a couple of shots aiming at where they'd last glimpsed their attackers. Granger heard Amy's lighter footsteps go down the short steps. Roberts's heavier steps followed for two steps, then stopped.

Granger didn't turn his head. 'Get goin', Morley,' he said.

Roberts said something that Granger didn't catch as Billy let off another shot, before they both reloaded as fast as they could from the shells on their belts. When Granger glanced around, the space around the trapdoor was empty.

'How many shells you got, Billy,' Granger asked.

'What I got on my belt.'

'Same here. We gotta make 'em all count now on.'

'Yeah,' Billy said quietly. Granger was aware that his stepbrother was looking across at him. Then Billy spoke again.

'You mind me askin' you somethin', Matt?' Billy hesitated for a moment before continuing. 'You ain't mad I never took your pa's name, are you?'

'Fer Chris'sakes, Billy! You sure do pick your time! No, I ain't mad, why should I be? Pa made a good marriage with your ma, an' he tol' me once 'bout Mr Haynes at Wilderness.' Granger looked across at Billy. 'Pa was good for this town, an' you gotta follow him.'

'I'm aimin' to do that.' Billy's mouth lifted. 'That's if we get outa here.'

'That's what I'm sayin', Billy. Your job's gonna be easier from now on. Ralston's finished, so is Johnny Mac. I'm the one they really want.'

Granger kept his eyes forward. 'Billy, you're goin' down the trapdoor.'

Startled, Billy's head shot around to glare across at Granger. 'I ain't doin' no such thing! You listen to me, Matt Granger! I'm the sheriff o' Springwater, an' don't you ferget it!'

'You stay, they're gonna kill us both, Billy! Ralston's got six men out there, lots of ammunition, an' lots of time.'

'You think our fathers would give up that easy?' Billy turned back to face across the street. 'I'm stayin', an' that's

141

an end to it.'

'I guess I had to— Jesus Christ!' Granger rolled from his kneeling position, and brought up his Navy at full arm's length as the slug from the long gun fired from the roof of the store opposite ploughed into the wooden board where a moment before he'd been kneeling. His Navy cracked once, cordite fumes rising from the barrel.

A long gun bounced once on the edge of the building opposite, turning in a cartwheel to clip the edge of the boardwalk and coming to rest in the dirt of Main Street. An instant later Granger caught a glimpse of a man falling headfirst, his arms outstretched. Granger heard the sound of his body thudding into the hardpack, and raised his head for a quick look. The man was still, blood beginning to stain the soil around him.

Billy, too, snatched a look. 'Odds are gettin' better all the time,' he said evenly. His voice roughened, suddenly. He must have spotted something.

'Matt! They're gonna rush us!'

'Everythin' you got, Billy!' Granger shouted. 'But steady!'

The two men came off their knees, half crouched, sidearms extended, firing repeatedly across the street, as bullets from four or five sidearms carried by the advancing men whistled around their heads. Granger swung his Navy, willing himself not to fire until he was sure of his aim. Halfway across the street the advancing line broke, three of the gunmen hit, the fourth shouting loudly, turned aside and ran from Granger's view. Almost simultaneously, the hammers of both their Navy Colts clicked on empty weapons. Granger snatched beneath his trail jacket for the hilt of his knife before realizing that the street had gone quiet.

Billy slumped down behind the metal of the broken

printing press breathing heavily, blood pouring from his arm, his sidearm falling to clatter on the boards.

'Goddamnit, Matt! I got hit!' Billy said between gritted teeth.

'Hold it there, Billy!' Granger said, frantically, pushing his last slugs into his Navy. Rearmed, he crawled across to Billy to inspect the wound. A close look and he was reassured.

'Straight through, an' it musta missed the bone.' He tore off his bandanna and wrapped it around Billy's arm. 'You shoot with your left?'

'Some. I ain't sure,' Billy said. 'Anyways, I got no slugs left.'

There was a shout of anger from across the street and then the beat of a horse's hoofs against the hardpack, fading away as the rider put distance between himself and the dead men in the street.

Granger breathed in deeply. It was the gunman he'd seen breaking the line, he reckoned. If he'd judged their numbers correctly that left only Ralston and Johnny Mac remaining across the street. Two against two. But there was nothing to gain by fooling himself. Whatever Ralston and Johnny Mac were, they weren't quitters. He had the six shots in his Navy, and that was all. Johnny Mac was as fast as all hell, and Ralston was known to practise his marksmanship every day. Six shots wouldn't take both of them.

His head jerked up as a thought came to him. 'Billy, the thirty-sixes you put in the livery stable the day they were gonna break out Zack Rudman. You pick 'em up agin?'

'I ain't given 'em a thought! They must be still there!'

'Would Wilkins have found 'em?'

Billy shook his head. 'I tucked 'em under some old canvas inside the side door. Canvas looked as if it had been there since the war.'

Granger did some quick thinking. The livery stable was maybe twenty yards from the door of the newspaper office. It could be the longest twenty yards he'd run all his life. If Billy could pin Ralston and Johnny Mac down long enough he might just reach those boxes of thirty-sixes.

He picked up Billy's sidearm, snapped open the chambers, and then did the same with his own Navy. Taking Billy's sidearm would have been quicker but he'd always followed one rule: *never trust a weapon you hadn't fired yourself.*

He loaded Billy's weapon, leaving one slug in his own Navy. His stepbrother's head was beginning to droop forward, his eyes closing, as the shock of his wound began to tell. Granger shook him roughly by his other arm.

'Hold on there, Billy!' he urged.

Billy shook his head, pushing himself up against the metal plate an inch.

'Ready, Matt,' he said.

Granger's lips twitched. Billy was barely conscious, unaware as yet of what his stepbrother was planning. But he was ready. Just like his father at Wilderness.

'I'm gonna go through the door, an' get to the livery,' he said. 'You're gonna have to keep their heads down. Soon as I open the door you start firin'. Do the best you can with your left hand. You got that?'

Billy nodded. 'Got it.'

Granger looked at him, his face grim. 'It's a gamble, Billy. You could end up with nothin' to shoot. An' if they let me run—'

'You'll be back to cover me,' interrupted Billy. He pushed against Granger's arm with his hand, and picked up his loaded Navy. He heaved around his body to prop his left hand holding the sidearm on the top edge of one of the metal plates. He turned his head to face the street.

144

'Get goin',' he said.

Granger belly-crawled across the room, making sure he kept behind the metal plates until he was a few feet from the door. He pushed himself into a crouch. Luckily the heaviness of the previous attacks had splintered the latch on the door, and Granger could see that one pull would be sufficient to open the door wide enough for him to pass through.

He leaned forward and gripped the edge of the door with his left hand while he held his Navy high. One shot would have to be enough to get him to the livery stable. He went through the route in his mind; out of the door, along the boardwalk, down the steps, across the alleyway, and through the small door at the corner of the barn.

He swallowed a couple of times. Ralston and Johnny Mac would have plenty of time to shoot him down although the shadows thrown on to the boardwalk would be a help. Still in a crouched position, he released the door and unstrapped his spurs; first the left, then changing his sidearm to the other hand, he slipped off the other from his right boot.

He took hold again of his Navy with his right hand, and reached forward again to grip the door. Deliberately, he sucked air deep into his lungs.

'OK, Billy!'

As the first shot rang out, Granger launched himself through the door and onto the boardwalk. From the corner of his eye he saw a shape move on the opposite side of the street. Two yards from the door, he swung sideways, brought up his Navy, and fired off a shot while he dashed along the boards, leaping over a basket that lay abandoned on the boards.

Shots thudded into the store fronts as he raced along, sending chips of wood flying, some shots behind him, some ahead. One shot was close enough for him to hear the whistle of air as it struck the board less than a couple of yards from his running feet. Behind him, he could hear the bark of shots from Billy, measured so as to conserve his remaining slugs.

He threw himself down the steps at the end of the boardwalk, aware now that he was protected by the heavy timbers at the corner of the building and launched himself against the door of the livery stable, bursting through and falling headlong on to the straw-covered earth.

He rolled across the ground, hands outstretched, groping beneath the canvas thrown into the corner of the barn. Thank God for Wilkins's lack of tidiness. His fingers closed around the boxes left by Billy. He jumped to his feet, clutching three boxes, moving quickly down the barn away from the door. There was no sign of Wilkins. Like the other townsfolk he must have made himself scarce.

Granger passed horses, snorting and stamping in their stalls, as he reloaded his Navy. Shoving the boxes into his trail coat, he spun around on his heel and moved back along the barn. He reached the door, his Navy held shoulder high. Should he risk crossing Main Street and taking Ralston and Johnny Mac from the rear? Or should he gamble on going back the way he'd come, and make a stand alongside Billy? Whatever he decided, he could now face Ralston and Johnny Mac. He had only one aim now, and that was to kill them both. He wondered how far Roberts had got with Amy. Once Amy was safe, he'd wager that Roberts would come hightailing back.

He pushed open the door, ready to make his decision. A voice rang out along Main Street. 'Matt! Can you hear me?'

Granger stood still, the door half open. He couldn't be

seen from the street but neither could he see what was happening along in front of the newspaper office. Again the voice rang out.

'Matt! It's Johnny Mac. Can you hear me?'

Granger froze. The direction of the sound meant that Macpherson had to be in the middle of the street. Billy was out of ammunition, or he was dead. What was Johnny Mac trying to set up? Was Ralston getting ready to shoot him down as soon as he stepped out from the livery barn?

'I hear you, Johnny Mac!' Granger called out.

'We gotta talk, Matt! This shootin's no damned good! Put down your gun an' step out so we can parlay.'

'I step out, an' Ralston bushwhacks me. That your plan, Johnny Mac?'

'Ralston's dead, Matt. That crazy stepbrother of yourn charged across the street, and shot him down.'

'An' you've killed Billy, I reckon.'

'You take me for a fool, Matt? I ain't crazy enough to kill a sheriff,' Macpherson shouted. 'Billy's passed out, an' I let him be. Now for Chris'sakes put down your gun an' come out an' talk.'

'You're wastin' your time, Johnny Mac,' Granger shouted. 'I'm comin' out, an' you an' me are gonna settle this once an' for all.'

He stepped out from behind the door, his Navy cocked and held just forward of his leg, ready to be brought to bear in any direction needed. The street was obscured by the heavy timbers on the corner of the end store and he moved to give himself a clear view along the street. Then he froze, swallowing fast as bile surged to the back of his throat.

Macpherson stood in the middle of the street, his right hand holding his Smith & Wesson against the head of Amy. His left hand was around her mouth, holding her hard against him, Amy's body providing him with a perfect shield. Granger felt his stomach muscles knot. Roberts had to be dead. The young Englishman would never have allowed Amy to be captured while there was a breath left in his body.

Granger eased the hammer of his Navy forward. Would Macpherson shoot him down like a dog if he threw his sidearm into the street? He walked forward, his Navy still held by his thigh, halting about ten feet from Amy. She was shaking, her face ashen, and her eyes were bulging with fear. Granger felt the fury burn throughout his whole body.

' 'Fraid that fancy talking Englishman didn't make it,' Macpherson said.

Still holding his sidearm hard against Amy's head, he slipped his hand from her mouth, now his need for her silence was over.

'Ralston killed him,' Amy choked out the words. 'He was waiting for us at the end of the alleyway.'

Granger nodded and stared directly at Macpherson. 'You threatenin' to kill innocent women now, Johnny Mac?' he said.

'I'm aimin' to ride outa here, Matt. Me an' Cora.'

'What about the Nugget?'

Macpherson shrugged. 'Cora's got our money stashed all over the country. The Nugget don't matter.'

Maybe Macpherson suddenly sensed that he was being cornered by Granger's even tone and the measured questions being put to him. The expression in his eyes hardened, and his face stiffened. When he spoke, his voice was harsh.

'You're gonna throw that Navy into the dust, or I swear I'll kill her.'

'An' then I'll kill you,' Granger said.

148

'Sure you will,' Macpherson said. 'An' you'll have the rest of your life to think about it. You really want that? Your woman's life against me an' Cora ridin' outa Springwater?' Macpherson said.

Silently, Granger stared at Macpherson for several seconds. Then his shoulders lifted an inch. What the hell! He'd come to Springwater to settle his father's affairs. That was all. He'd been damned lucky to meet Amy and if he hadn't been so hellfire bent on going after Ralston, she wouldn't have been put in danger not just once but twice. Now Roberts had paid the ultimate price, and what he'd heard about Billy didn't sound good.

He cursed inwardly. Why was there always someone around telling him all he had to do was to kill another couple of men and all the problems would be solved? To hell with it! Macpherson could be bluffing. But was he going to take a chance? Amy's life was worth a thousand times any notion he might have of revenging Charlie, or even Pa, or putting Billy on the right path.

A smile began to spread across Macpherson's face, as if he could read the thoughts going through Granger's mind. He watched as Granger turned and tossed his Navy into the dirt.

'An' the knife, Matt,' Macpherson said.

Granger reached below the sleeve of his trail jacket, and pulled out his knife. He tossed it into the dirt.

'Let her go,' he said.

'Sure,' Macpherson said. He pushed Amy aside, sending her tottering for a few steps before she sprawled headlong in the dirt.

Granger took a step in her direction.

'As stupid as Charlie,' Macpherson said. He brought up his sidearm, already cocked.

'You sonovabitch!' Granger yelled.

He kicked upwards, the sharp toe of his boot smashing into the underside of Macpherson's wrist. The gun barrel pointed skywards as the trigger was pulled, sending the slug past Granger's shoulder, as the weapon spun from Macpherson's hand. Granger's bunched fist smashed into Macpherson's face, driving him back, and Granger hurled himself forward, his fists flailing.

Macpherson was fast and for a man who spent hours at the card table, in good shape. His arms came up in turn to parry Granger's blows, and he kicked out at Granger catching him on the knee, stopping Granger's forward lunge.

Macpherson jumped back, free for a moment to reach inside his coat, but with his hand maybe trapped in a pocket, he was unable to parry the swing of Granger's fist. His breath hit Granger's face, and Granger's knuckles sank into Macpherson's silk vest. Macpherson, hand held to his middle, turned and staggered three or four paces down the street, as if he was about to fall.

'You're gonna hang, you murderin' bastard!'

Macpherson turned, his face puce, spittle showing at the corner of his mouth. Yet his eyes shone with triumph. He brought his hand from beneath his jacket, and levelled the pocket revolver at Granger's head.

'I got five shots, an' I'm gonna kill your woman next,' he snarled.

Granger saw the mouth of the .31 Colt aimed directly at his head. The black hole seemed as big as a Johnny Reb cannon. There was the crack of gunfire. For a moment the two men stood suspended, then Macpherson folded at the knees, pitched face forward into the dust and lay still.

Twenty yards along the street Cora stood opposite the newspaper office by the bodies of Ralston's men. In her hands she held a long gun. As Granger watched he saw the rifle drop to the boards, and her head thrown back. He stood still as Cora's howl of pain and anguish rang down the street, raising the hairs on the back of his neck.

CHAPTER FIFTEEN

It was late in the morning when the two sombrely dressed men appeared at the door of the newspaper office. They stood on the threshold while the four men delivering the new printing press from Cheyenne promised they'd be back after noon to finish the job.

'Two or three days, Mrs Morgan, an' the paper'll be back on the street,' said the dark-featured man who'd been supervising the work.

After the four had left, Granger stepped forward to welcome the two Quakers to the office. 'We've been expecting you, gentlemen,' Granger said, waving them in the direction of the two chairs set by Amy's desk.

'Thank you, Mr Granger,' said the taller of the two.

Both men doffed their broad-brimmed hats as they stepped into the office. Unlike the grey shirts on the bodies of the two men he and Amy had seen, these men wore white cotton shirts beneath their black coats. The two men bowed when Granger introduced them to Amy as 'Mrs Amy Granger, the owner and editor of the *Reporter*'.

After everyone was seated the taller man introduced himself and his companion. 'I am John Fox, and my colleague here is Henry Brambell,' he said. 'Before we speak of business, Mr Granger, I would like to thank thee for seeing our two brothers laid to rest in a manner they would have wished.'

Granger shifted in his chair. 'That was more Sheriff Haynes' doin', Mr Fox. I just lent a hand.'

A gentle smile appeared on the face of Fox. 'I'm not sure if Sheriff Haynes could have paid the various bills, Mr Granger. Thou art truly blessed.'

Again Granger shifted in his chair, glancing at Amy. How could he explain that he'd been given back a thousand dollars by Cora who now owned the town's saloon? Better Mr Fox didn't know the money came from gambling tables and the activities of hurdy-gurdy girls.

'I was glad to help,' he said.

'General Parker wishes me to convey his sincere sympathy for the loss of your father,' said Fox. 'Without Mr Granger's efforts, and his contacts with the Shoshone, we may never have discovered the truth. We now know that Thomas Ralston illegally took possession of the land almost twenty years ago. That was land meant for homesteaders.'

'You mean Ralston just upped an' stole it?'

'I'm sorry to say that's exactly what he did,' Fox said.

'But how was he ever able to steal so much land?' Amy asked.

'Thomas Ralston had been a senior official in the Indian Bureau. He used his position to alter documents, issue false orders, and when he was certain of his position he resigned from the bureau, and came out West.'

Fox sighed deeply. 'Regrettably, the bureau has a history of corruption. But President Grant has appointed General Parker to restore its good name.' Fox's gentle smile reappeared 'The General has kindly chosen the Friends to assist him.'

'The so-called "Quaker Policy", Mr Fox,' Amy said. 'I've been reading about it.'

153

'I believe some of the newspapers back East are calling it that,' said Brambell, speaking for the first time.

'One question keeps nagging at me, Mr Fox,' Granger said. 'How did my father know the general well enough to receive letters from him?'

'Forgive me, Mr Granger, I assumed you knew,' Fox said. 'Your father served with the general during the war. General Parker was with the engineers.'

'But why should the general go back to using his tribal name for his letters?'

It was Brambell's turn to show Granger and Amy a smile. 'The general used it during the war among his officers to guard certain information. Your father must have known that. The general received your father's first letter the day he took up his appointment. At that time he wasn't sure who he could trust in the bureau.'

'What happens now?' Granger asked.

'Lawyers from the East will soon be here. Eventually the land will be taken by homesteaders. Springwater will prosper, although sadly the Lazy Y cowboys will be out of work.'

'But there's good news from east of here, Mr Fox,' Granger said. 'The English lord, Frewen, is buyin' more stock, an' he's lookin' for men.'

Fox stood up from his chair, Brambell following suit. 'Then we can return to Cheyenne and report good news, Mr Granger.' He picked up his broad-brimmed hat from the desk. 'We'll bid you good day, ma'am, Mr Granger. The Good Lord has surely smiled on you both.'

Both Granger and Amy were silent for a few moments after the two men had left. The two Quakers had made Granger realize that his father had never spoken much about the war. Instead he had preferred to sit around, smoking his favourite pipe, drinking his coffee 'made strong so the spoon stands up straight'.

'I'm gonna find out what Pa an' his engineers did in the War,' Granger said suddenly, and a mite too loudly. Embarrassment showed briefly on his face. 'An' I'm gonna have him moved from the hill to the old place now Jack an' Katy are back there.'

He stood up. 'Those fellers from Cheyenne have done a good job.'

Amy nodded. 'They'll have the press running tomorrow. I'll work all night if needs be. Morley is sorely missed,' she added soberly. 'He could have written his piece as if for the *Boston Globe* and I'd still have sold more papers than ever before.'

The door banged and Granger turned to see Billy Haynes at the threshold, his shirt sleeve bulging above his bandaged gunshot wound. His face was red with excitement and he was scarcely able to get his words out, as he stepped into the *Reporter's* premises.

'Matt! Across the office, you're needed now!'

There was a cry of anguish from Amy, who clutched on to Granger's arm. 'No, Billy! Enough! Matthew has done enough for the town!'

Billy was almost hopping from foot to foot in his excitement. 'No, Miss Amy! Nothin's goin' on! You folks wouldna guess who's across there, an' he's askin' for you, Matt.'

'Governor of the Territory?' Granger suggested with a grin.

Billy shook his head so strongly Granger wondered if his stepbrother would fall over. 'No! A much more important feller.' Billy took a deep breath. 'General Grenville Dodge, builder of the railroad. He didn't even go to the hotel when he got off the stage.' Billy's chest swelled visibly. 'Came straight to my office an' asked for me by name.'

Granger, amused by Billy's display of pride, looked at Amy.

'Sounds as though we're bein' summoned by this great man.'

He crossed the office to pick up the basket prepared that morning by Polly. If anything, it was heavier than the one she'd made up for a day that would for ever remain in his memory. He picked up the keys from the desk and held out his arm to Amy.

'Do we go to the Majestic?' he asked Billy.

'He's gonna wait in the office, drinkin' coffee off my stove like a regular feller.' Billy held up his hand and waved. 'Follow me!'

Billy opened the door, allowing Granger and Amy to step past into his office. As he did so, the tall man, wearing a grey Prince Albert, placed his mug of coffee on the desk and rose from his chair.

Dodge stepped forward and bowed to Amy. 'Mrs Morgan, I assume. I'm delighted to meet you.'

A surprised Amy managed to say, 'Thank you,' as Dodge moved forward to provide her with his chair, pausing a moment while she settled her skirts. Then he looked up at Granger and held out his hand.

'Good to see you again, Matt,' he said.

Granger put down the basket and grasped his hand. 'An' good to see you, General. It's been some time.'

Billy's jaw dropped open; Amy's eyes widened in surprise.

'You know each other?' Amy asked.

Dodge chuckled. 'Matt worked for me for several years until those cunning bankers back East offered him more money than I could match.'

'That reminds me,' Granger said. He dug his hand into

156

a pocket and pulled out the badge he'd worn the first day he'd acted as Billy's deputy. 'I should have returned this when I left.'

Dodge glanced down at the badge with its insignia *Chief of Detectives*, and shook his head. 'Keep it, Matt. You earned it many times. And that reminds me,' he added. He looked around at Billy, who was standing rigid by the door, as if spellbound by what was happening in his office.

'I hear good things about you, Sheriff,' Dodge said. 'Write me a letter next year. I always need good men.'

Dodge looked up at the old railway clock. 'They'll have changed the horses by now, so I must leave.' He turned to Granger. 'I'm on my way to discuss business with the English lord, Frewen, to the east. UP has agreed to build a spur to his land. Once it's built he'll not need to drive his cattle south to the railhead.'

He shook hands with Grange and bowed to Amy. 'I understand you and Matt are shortly to be wed. He's a most fortunate man, and I offer my best wishes. I know the bankers back East think highly of Matt.'

'I'm quitting the banks, I wrote them yesterday,' Granger said.

Dodge looked up quickly. 'I can match their money now, Matt.'

Granger, smiling, shook his head. 'I'm trying a new venture,' he said.

He stepped across to stand beside Amy. 'Times are changin', an' I've been carryin' a gun too long. I'm gonna try my hand at the newspaper business.'

Dodge smiled, 'Maybe I should have guessed. I'm sure you'll do well.'

He bowed again in Amy's direction, shook the hands of the two men, and stepped through the door held open by Billy.

The moment the door had closed Billy jigged half-a-dozen steps on the spot. 'Jumpin' rattlesnakes! Did you hear what he said?'

Granger laughed. 'You gonna be a UP man next year, Billy?'

Billy stopped jigging around, his expression serious. 'Nope. I gotta town to look after.' Then a wide grin split his face. 'But I'm sure glad to be asked.'

Granger picked up the basket he'd carried from the newspaper office.

'Time we all went down town,' he said.

'Miss Amy, Mr Granger, Sheriff Haynes! Good to see you all,' Dr Simmons said, as they reached the open door of his clapboard house that stood at the edge of town. Simmons must have seen them push open the white-painted gate a few yards along a path of small stones. Simmons looked at the basket in Granger's hand, and smiled.

'If I know Miss Amy and her Polly there's a real feast in there,' he said.

'You've earned it, Doc, an' more.'

'Truth be told, Mr Granger, there's been more luck in this terrible situation than medical science. But follow me.'

Amy and Granger followed the doctor through a short passageway where all three halted briefly at the door. Simmons turned as if to say something to Amy but he must have seen something in her eyes. Instead, he turned back to the door and pushed it open. As he did so, Amy gripped hard on Granger's elbow.

In the corner of the room Morley Roberts lay in bed propped against pillows, sheets pulled up only as far as his midriff. Above the sheets Granger could see Roberts's chest covered with black bruises spreading across from armpit to armpit. On his left side a bandage was tied around his shoulder, a small circle of blood showing at its centre.

A gasp of shock came from Amy, and Roberts opened his eyes. 'Matt, Miss Amy,' Roberts said, his voice stronger than Granger had expected.

'We've brought you an' Doc some food,' Granger said, holding up the basket.

'Little Polly, I wager,' said Roberts, managing a smile.

'Truly a miracle,' said Simmons. 'The good Lord surely didn't want Mr Roberts just yet.'

Amy sat carefully on the end of the bed. 'I thought you were dead, Morley.'

'Never underestimate the power of literature, Miss Amy,' he said. Amused by their puzzled expressions, he looked at Simmons. 'Show them, Doctor.'

Simmons moved to the small cabinet beside the bed and opened the top drawer. From it he took a small fat, leather-backed book which Granger immediately recognized as one of the books in which Roberts was for ever making notes.

Simmons held up the book. 'Truly a miracle,' he said.

Granger saw that plumb in the centre of the book's front cover was a clean hole. Simpson opened the book and there, buried in between the pages was a bullet. He turned the book around to show the nose of the bullet, showing brown stains, barely protruding from the leather cover.

'It's truly a miracle,' repeated Amy. 'How long before Mr Roberts can come home?' she asked.

'A week at the most,' Simmons replied. 'A couple of weeks rest after, and he'll be fit for the long journey back to England.'

Granger looked at the Englishman, keeping his face straight. 'You ain't gonna be bored, are you, Morley? All the no-goods dead, or in Billy's jailhouse.'

'I'm thinking about my book,' Roberts said.

'Have you a title yet?' Amy asked.

Roberts's face showed a wry smile. 'I think I may call it *Western Avernus.*'

Amy burst out with laughter. 'Honestly, Morley!' she exclaimed. 'You and your beloved classics!'

'You gonna let us all in on this?' Granger asked, mystified by the amused expressions on their two faces.

'Morley's book title!' Amy exclaimed. 'The Western Gate to Hell!' For a moment there was total silence and then, as Amy took Roberts's hand, and Granger put his arm around Billy's shoulders, the room echoed with the sounds of their laughter.